THE
SONGBIRD
GIRLS

BOOKS BY RICHARD PARKER

THE DETECTIVE TOM FABIAN SERIES

Never Say Goodbye
The Songbird Girls

Keep Her Safe
Hide and Seek
Follow You

Scare Me
Stop Me
Stalk Me

THE SONGBIRD GIRLS

RICHARD PARKER

bookouture

Published by Bookouture in 2018

An imprint of StoryFire Ltd.

Carmelite House
50 Victoria Embankment
London EC4Y 0DZ

www.bookouture.com

ISBN: 978-1-78681-788-4
eBook ISBN: 978-1-78681-787-7

To my fine friend Chuck Cartmel and his family.
Here's to another quarter of a century for you and Bob.

CHAPTER ONE

Parents' meeting. Horror. Polly had highlighted the date with a green luminous marker on her kitchen calendar the day she'd been given it and had counted down the days since the beginning of the week. She'd missed the last one and the guilt and shame had been magnified by the stiff letter she'd had from Logan's form tutor informing her just how compunctious she should have been.

But there were so many dates to log at the beginning of each term – sports extension evenings, choir rehearsals, outings, inset days – and Polly miraculously fitted her dog-walking business around every one of them. She had been determined not to miss the next parents' meeting, however. Had ensured she had only one client booking early that afternoon and that she had plenty of time to drive to St Jude's.

But her smugness had evaporated after a bus had broken down on Garratt Lane and she'd spent an hour crawling through Earlsfield, willing the traffic on and anticipating the disapproving faces that would be waiting to greet her in the assembly hall.

The clock on the dash seemed to have moved on a minute every time she looked at it as she perched on the edge of her seat, willing the cars ahead to surge forward. This was the only route she could take so she had no choice but to sit and wait. It was Halloween. The kids were having a party first. Maybe that would run over.

She took out her mobile. Phone ahead. Let them know what was going on. Other parents would be having the same issue. She was about to dial when the traffic rolled forward and she had to accelerate to keep up. Was it about to stall again? But the cars kept moving and soon she was swerving around the offending double-decker and picking up speed towards the primary school.

Minutes later she turned right at the red bricked façade of St Jude's. Pumpkins glowed in the hall window. Polly readied herself for the next gauntlet – finding a parking space. This was difficult enough on any day at three in the afternoon but as the building next door was being renovated behind polythene sheeting and there were several skips positioned in the bay usually clogged up with parents' off-road vehicles it was going to be even more of a free-for-all than usual.

But she had one advantage – a Golf. And Polly had learned to fit it into the tightest spaces. She surged to the end of the road and spied a space at the end just in front of the entrance to the railway bridge steps.

Shit. It was excruciatingly too small. Then she acknowledged that there was somebody sitting inside the blue Toyota SUV in front of the space. It was a male with broad shoulders and her blood boiled as she noted his car had a large gap in front of it and that his vehicle was taking up two spaces.

Polly beeped her horn.

The man didn't even turn around.

She honked again and watched his head tilt up to his mirror. He didn't appear in any hurry to move though.

Polly was about to blast the horn again when his engine started and he leisurely rolled his Toyota forward. But he still left himself plenty of space at the front, which meant she had to carefully manoeuvre her Golf up to his bumper and almost scrape hers on the bollard behind her.

'Moron.' But it was eight minutes past three and she had no time to waste.

He got out of his car the same time as her and didn't even turn back. Was he one of the parents? She didn't recognise him from the rear.

He strode off in the direction of the high street and she followed, determined to make it into the hall before ten past and join the queue for Mr Appleton. Maybe she'd throw a remark at the space hogger on her way past.

When steel struck the back of her head, Polly's brain briefly took her to a safe place. She thought she was sitting at home in her armchair, the lounge quiet except for the clock ticking. The sensations of the cushion beneath her seemed so real but consciousness and reality surged quickly back.

A clatter.

Polly looked down at her new trainers. There was blood on the pristine white toes. Next to her feet was a ball peen hammer and that had blood on it as well. Where the hell was she? The street was still visible but looked smudged. She realised she was behind the polythene sheeting of the scaffolding on the building next door to the school.

She tried to scream, to alert the man who had got out of the Toyota but a hand was over her nose and mouth and her panicked exclamation was held inside her head.

But the man was coming back and she yelled as hard as she could against a hot palm, felt it vibrate through the veins in her temples.

Polly could feel warmth at the back of her head and guessed it was where she'd been hit with the hammer.

The man stopped at his car, opened the door at the back, extracted a sports bag he'd forgotten and closed it again. He was only about twelve feet away from her, and just a cloudy sheet of polythene concealed her. Polly fought to cry out again.

She felt a sharp jab to the right side of her spine and her strangled howl was abruptly cut off.

Another harsh pain in her back and this time the agony went much deeper.

The man marched away but she couldn't form another sound.

Polly tried to struggle against the figure securing her from behind but felt her strength quickly ebb. But all she was thinking about was Logan waiting for her with his tutor.

When would they find her here?

CHAPTER TWO

NINE DAYS EARLIER

The dirty sandstone outer wall of Kerslake Prison was seemingly endless as Detective Inspector Tom Fabian directed his green Audi around its curve and struggled to keep to the thirty limit. As the road straightened out he slipped in his Bluetooth earpiece and rang Harriet's number.

She picked up after three rings. 'You're late then.'

He looked at the digital clock on the dash. 'Only by quarter of an hour.'

'Deliberately?'

She knew him too well. Which is probably why they were separated. But he'd told Harriet where he was going and she knew how apprehensive he'd be.

Three years ago Fabian had put Christopher Wisher, infamous London serial killer, behind bars. He'd murdered nine people. Mutilated them in a way only he understood. Fabian could still remember his last victim, Justine Kavanagh. As well as subjecting her body to the same evisceration as the previous eight victims he'd also caved her head in with her own kitchen chopping board.

'I don't feel like being punctual.' But he felt like he'd been summonsed. Wisher had said he would only talk to Fabian but had refused to say what it was in relation to. DCI Metcalfe, his boss, had told Fabian he had to visit him at the prison at 'his nearest convenience.' Fabian's or Wisher's?

And Metcalfe had taken great delight in insisting. Fabian knew he resented the way he'd handled the investigation in 2015 because he'd involved the media. A BBC show, *Urban Predator*, that had been tailing Fabian before he was assigned the case had captured every stage of the inquiry and when they'd done a TV reconstruction and appeal for witnesses an anonymous caller had given them the break they needed. The caller had used a phone box near to Wisher's home and had never been traced. The show had won its producer, Angelina Friedmann, an award as well as a promotion; Metcalfe remained suspicious that she still had Fabian's ear. He hadn't spoken to her since the end of the trial, however. Not even when the show had been aired.

'Don't let him back in your head.' Harriet knew about the interrogations Fabian had conducted with Wisher.

'I don't like that I've had to drop everything to be here. If this is just Wisher craving the spotlight I'll send him straight back to his cell.'

'You really think that's the case?'

'It's exactly three years to the day since Wisher started his sentence.'

Fabian didn't want to share a room with Wisher again but there *was* a chance he could close a few cold cases in the Richmond area. That's why Metcalfe had been so eager to dispatch him there. Even though Wisher had readily confessed to nine murders there was always a chance he could be responsible for more. There were no bodies on file with similar mutilations to Wisher's victims but that wasn't to say he couldn't be responsible for myriad missing persons. Wisher knew that, which was why he'd been economical with his reasons for his audience with Fabian. He doubted Wisher had withheld from him three years ago, but he had no choice other than to attend.

Fabian approached the metallic grey panelled gates and he slowed the car. 'Heard from Tilly?'

'Yesterday lunchtime.'

His daughter had just started her first term at Exeter University and he knew she'd already found a guy she was interested in. That had happened in the first week which Fabian thought was way too quick. Things had gone quiet since, though. 'Any mention of Mark?'

'No. She's playing her cards close to her chest.'

'Let's hope so.'

Fabian showed his ID to the guy in the security booth and he opened the gates. He waited as they swung out to admit him and the foreboding grey brick edifice of the east wing came into view against the dingy afternoon sky. Like many in the country Kerslake Prison was overcrowded, financially in dire straits and things were going to get a lot worse before they got any better.

'Are you there on your own?' She didn't answer straight away and he immediately regretted the question.

'Yes,' she replied warily.

He imagined Harriet, her tight brown curls wrapped in one of her bright silk headscarves, cross-legged on the old couch in the back dining room lounge with only Bacardi the cat for company.

'I didn't mean…' It was none of his business. Fabian knew there was a new guy, Martin, in her life. It was still early days but he wondered how long it would be before he moved into the home he'd used to inhabit. 'Have you had a square meal since Tilly left?'

'Yes.' But there was affection in the defensive retort.

'Eating at Spigo's doesn't count.'

His maisonette was only a stone's throw from her. He knew how lucky he was to still be able to drop into the house to occasionally cook dinner for her and Tilly and at least pretend that the hours he spent there were like old family time. How much longer could that last, though? Tilly had more or less left home so now there was going to be less friction if Harriet did want someone to start staying there. But it was her property. Fabian contributed but Harriet's job with the MOD meant she could comfortably support herself.

'If you need to talk when you're on your way back…'

Fabian rolled onto the tarmac-paved car park. 'I'll be fine. Look, I've got to sign in now. I'll speak to you soon.'

'OK. Good luck.' Harriet hung up before he did.

In the past his job meant a lot of snatched calls to Harriet to make excuses for his absence and now the instant hang-up was her control.

Fabian pulled the Audi into a space and then strode across the car park through the drizzle to sign in at the visitors' reception, his circulation thudding in one ear. He waited for his heart murmur, the stumbling double flutter that his doctor had told him was a common complaint even for people younger than forty-four. The accelerated beat had become a constant presence.

The elderly uniformed officer sniffed intermittently as Fabian filled out the form. 'I'm to extend you every hospitality, according to Governor Briant.' He didn't sound like he was happy about that at all.

Fabian was led down a corridor with dark blue doors off it. He saw his own prematurely white hair lit and reflected in the reinforced glass of the double locked doors that led to the visitors' room. As the stocky guard with the shaved head on the other side peered through it looked like it was his. It suited him better. He buzzed Fabian through.

'Another visitor for Wisher?' The guard held the door open and stood back. 'He has a busier social life than I do.'

Fabian nodded at him and swallowed dryly as he was admitted.

CHAPTER THREE

The guard showed Fabian to an orange plastic seat at a table in the small square room that smelt strongly of bleach and body odour. One wall was bars and the guard nodded at the other uniformed sentry behind them who trudged off, keys jingling with each step.

Fabian seated himself at the table. 'Who's been visiting him?' he asked the remaining guard. Fabian knew Wisher's immediate family had disowned him after the trial. Why hadn't any close friends emerged in the inquiry?

'His fan club. There's always somebody who wants to interview him for their blog and Wisher never turns down an opportunity to talk about himself.'

Fabian knew there were certain serial killers who attained cult status but had always thought it to be more of an American phenomenon. But the fact that Wisher's crimes had received such wide media exposure was largely down to him, Angelina Friedmann and *Urban Predator*. 'What sort of prisoner is he?'

'Exemplary… till August last year.'

'What happened?'

The guard chewed at something. 'You'd better ask the governor that. Don't think Mr Wisher is happy with us any more,' he said derisively. 'Had his eye on a move to Bicknell Psychiatric.'

Bicknell was a modern facility that had only recently been built. The prisoners were all lifers who submitted to psychoanalysis programmes in return for better conditions.

'Had?'

'He's stopped talking about it now. Maybe because he knows the governor is never going to make the recommendation.'

'Why not?'

'From what I hear, the governor has been stonewalling Wisher since he started his sentence.'

Part of Fabian was glad to hear it. After murdering seven women and two men Fabian hated the idea of Wisher inveigling his way into a cushy deal at Bicknell Psychiatric.

'You've got to be pleased about that surely? You put him in here.'

Fabian often forgot how well known he'd become because of Angelina Friedmann's show. He nodded. But he'd heard great things about the programme at Bicknell. If Wisher's input would increase the understanding of his psyche, would that lead to earlier prevention of men like him preying on others? 'It's never going to happen?'

'Not while Briant's in the post.'

'Any idea why he won't entertain it?'

The guard shrugged. 'Who cares? Just as long as Wisher slums it here with us, I'm more than happy.'

Both their heads turned as they heard the jingling keys return.

It had been three years but Christopher Wisher looked a lot older. His tight curls were still jet black but his round features looked a little thinner and more anaemic. Fabian felt a sensation that he hadn't experienced since the last time he'd seen him, bubbles of unease slowly rising as they had done throughout every interview at Horseferry Police Station.

Wisher had never protested his innocence. He'd confessed to all nine murders on the day Fabian had arrested him. Hadn't objected to Angelina Friedmann shooting every moment. Had carried on as if the crew hadn't been hovering there and never once acknowledged them. It was as if he'd expected them to be in tow, that his crimes would have required nothing less.

Fabian had sat opposite Wisher in interview room 4 while he'd politely relayed his deeds in painstaking detail, almost as if it was a generous courtesy he'd extended to Fabian. Apologising when he briefly struggled to recall a time or date, calling on the minutiae of his homicides like the two of them were on a nostalgic journey.

But it was his own responses that unsettled Fabian. As a homicide detective, he knew how to be removed, how to coax with tact and civility. But Wisher made the process so easy for him that he could hear the gratitude in his own voice. Wisher had ignored Fabian's co-interrogator, Detective Sergeant Natasha Banner. Blanked everyone else in the room. His eyes had been locked only on Fabian.

It had felt like they were becoming friends and that's what had disturbed Fabian the most: the idea that they had any sort of connection.

Wisher didn't look through the bars as he was escorted to the door. His jade green overalls looked a little baggy on his emaciated frame. He was average build, average height. Average everything. And his thick-lensed spectacles made him seem even less threatening. It was a disarming countenance for a sociopath that had killed for no evident reason other than amusement. At least, that was the conclusion of everyone who had evaluated Wisher.

There were no significant episodes in his past that would even begin to explain the things he'd done. He was from a stable, middle class family background, married with one son and had worked for the civil service since his early twenties. He was thirty-nine the day he'd murdered his first victim, a young mother named Sonia Walker, in broad daylight in a family picnic park.

The guard was close behind him and they both halted at the door.

Wisher sharply turned his body, military style. The guard sighed.

Fabian noticed Wisher had an A4 notebook with a blue cover tucked under his left arm. Wisher met Fabian's gaze with his magnified dark brown eyes and he suppressed a shudder as he recalled how inculpably they'd blinked as he'd recounted his acts of violence.

The guard unlocked and opened the door.

Fabian wanted the meeting over. As soon as possible. Let Wisher say whatever he needed and let him know in no uncertain terms that unless he was offering something concrete he wasn't going to be indulged.

'You got what you wanted,' the guard with Wisher said.

Wisher didn't register the comment or the other guard in the room. His eyes remained on Fabian. His demeanour was relaxed, as if he'd only just sat with Fabian in interview room 4 the day before and not three years ago. He moved to his side of the table, gently placed the notebook in front of him and seated himself on the plastic orange chair with a bump.

The guard that had escorted him left and locked the door again and Fabian nodded at the other guard. He reversed but remained in the doorway they'd entered by. When he returned his gaze to Wisher he was rubbing the back of his neck. It was what he did when he was nervous; when Fabian's questions had focussed on anything but the mechanics of what he'd done. Wisher was always comfortable with 'how' but never 'why'.

'What's wrong?' Fabian immediately regretted gauging his mood. He'd told himself he'd remain entirely removed from their exchange.

Wisher darted his eyes left to the guard at the doorway. 'D'you think he'd rather be sat with us?' He said it conspiratorially but just loud enough for him to hear.

He'd immediately acted as he had during their previous conversations, made Fabian feel like it was the two of them against everyone else in the room. Fabian nodded again at the guard and he stepped out of the room.

Wisher inhaled through his nostrils as if steeling himself to say something more. But he just fixed Fabian.

'Shall we get to it?' Fabian needed to break the silence.

Wisher smirked slightly. Saw that he was uncomfortable. 'I've got something for you.'

Fabian's eyes dipped briefly to the notebook on the table. 'I was told you wanted to make a statement.'

'I do. This is it.' He didn't look down at the book.

'But you wanted to speak specifically to me.'

'I did. Wanted to make sure you got it. Personally.' He said the word precisely.

'What is it?'

'A journal. I'd like you to read it.'

'Why?'

Wisher looked a little hurt. 'I started work on it three years ago to this day. Say you'll read it.'

Fabian nodded. So the anniversary *was* significant. 'Anything else you want to discuss?'

'Everything I want to convey to you is in there.' Wisher put his forefinger on the cover of the notebook and slid it across the table-top.

Fabian put his fingertips on the cover and tried to drag it towards him.

But Wisher's finger remained there, pinning it down. After a few seconds he lifted it an inch away.

Fabian slid the book towards himself.

Wisher smiled with relief and sat back. 'Thank you.'

'What have I got here?' Fabian didn't open the notebook but noticed his name had been scrawled at the bottom of the cover.

'Thoughts.'

'I hear you're interested in moving to Bicknell. Would this not be invaluable to them?'

Wisher blinked and his glasses magnified his lashes. 'I'm no longer interested in Bicknell.'

'You've given up?'

'It's a pointless ambition.'

'Because of the governor's stance?'

'No. My needs have changed.'

'How?'

'I just want you to promise me you'll read the journal. That's it.'

'I won't make any promises.'

'I'm sure your job will dictate you do.'

Fabian nodded. 'There's nothing else?'

'No. Maybe we can just shoot the breeze for a while, though. Like we used to in the interview room. Harmless chit chat.' He enunciated again. 'I've missed your company. You can catch me up on your career since you arrested me. How's the family?'

Although the inquiry was convivial Fabian knew Wisher was provoking him.

'Harriet? Tilly?' Wisher raised his eyebrows.

Fabian refused to give Wisher the satisfaction of a facial reaction. How could he have known the names of his wife and daughter? He'd always sheltered them from media exposure. But if Wisher had been receiving guests the information could easily have been passed to him. 'Nothing else to add?'

Wisher approximated hurt. 'We don't have to talk about them.'

'Nothing else to add that's relevant to my visit?'

Wisher shook his head slightly. 'It good to see you again. Really. You look well. And I assume you're very busy. You have the journal. I won't detain you any longer. Wisher extended his hand to shake Fabian's. 'Except… you always listened to me. Intently.'

Fabian didn't know how to react.

'Are you still listening?'

Fabian looked at his palm but remained still.

The guard re-entered through the doorway.

'Retrospection. One word. That's your saving grace. But not indefinitely.' Wisher still had his hand out. His expectant expression unchanged.

Fabian stood, picked up the notebook but focussed on the exit. 'Take care, Tom.'

Fabian had never offered his Christian name to Wisher during questioning. Because of his TV profile, however, it was common knowledge and the serial killer had used it from the day he'd been arrested. Fabian walked out of the room and didn't look back at him.

CHAPTER FOUR

'Thanks for finding time.' Matt Briant gestured to one of two chairs in front of his desk.

Fabian had been surprised to get the summons from the governor before he'd left the prison and saw him eye the A4 notebook in his hand before he took a seat in the generous but minimalist office.

'Your meeting with Wisher was brief?' Briant sat down.

It sounded to Fabian like Briant already knew it had been. He waited to be told why he'd taken such an interest in his visit.

'If I'm honest, I just wanted to meet the officer who delivered Christopher to me.'

How old was Briant? Early thirties? Seemed too young to be in his position. Looked like he spent a lot of time on personal grooming. His glossy dark hair was shaved at the sides and longer on top and his nails were immaculate.

Briant swiped the overhang of fringe from his eyes and squared a stack of files on his desk. 'I understand he gave you something.' This time, he didn't acknowledge the notebook on Fabian's lap.

'Think I may have had a wasted journey.'

'Maybe so. I've read it, of course.' Briant still didn't look at it. Fabian was taken aback.

'I wouldn't have allowed it otherwise.'

Fabian gripped the edge of the notebook and felt slightly cheated. 'And what was *your* verdict?'

'There's not much in those pages that bears any resemblance to reality.'

Fabian realised why he was having the conversation. 'So does it contain any significantly negative experiences in Kerslake Prison?'

Briant briefly narrowed his eyes. 'See for yourself,' he said dismissively. 'Wisher's grasp on reality has become tenuous to say the least.'

But Fabian knew Wisher could interact with reality. He'd convincingly led an unremarkable middle class existence during the eight-month period he was preying on people. It was justifying why he mutilated his victims that he had never been drawn on. 'There's nothing there that will paint Kerslake in a bad light?'

'If there was d'you think I'd release the notebook to you? No, as you read on you'll realise that Wisher has entirely submitted to fantasy.'

It didn't sound like the man Fabian had just spoken to.

'If you think there's any worth in what he's written I'd be interested in you feeding back but I do think it's the product of his inability to cope with his confinement.'

'Has there been a marked change in his personality?'

Briant opened his mouth to reply but paused. 'Wisher keeps to himself and I believe that's the problem. Deprived of the normal family life he was always able to fall back on I think the delusional ego that allowed him to murder has now completely asserted itself.'

'Is that an official diagnosis?'

'Doctor Irvine is the therapist handling Wisher. She says he's becoming less and less forthcoming.'

'And what about the people who visit him? He still agrees to see *them*.'

'He's had visitors but because their interest is only in his crimes they simply feed his ego.'

'Is this not something you'd consider to be of interest to Bicknell?'

Briant's features hardened. 'Are you speaking on his behalf?'

'No. He didn't mention it to me. I just wondered if you think he's a candidate.'

Briant regarded him suspiciously. 'I've discussed it with Doctor Irvine. She doesn't think Wisher fits Bicknell's criteria.'

'Why not?'

'Says he's unresponsive to therapy. Only tells her what she wants to hear. That hasn't changed for three years. He's devious. Attacked her with his cuffs.'

'And she's still his doctor?' Fabian reacted incredulously.

'Yes.'

'Her first name?'

'Christine.'

Fabian made a mental note.

'I trust her instincts and she's recommended he remains at Kerslake for the foreseeable.'

Fabian had no desire to see Wisher get an easier ride but wondered if his being retained at Kerslake was simply a punishment.

'You can speak to her about it if you like. She's not in surgery today, though.'

Fabian shook his head. 'I've got more than enough on my plate at the moment. This has already taken too big a bite from my day.'

Briant nodded. 'He still talks about you.'

Fabian paused as he rose from his chair.

'Often mentions you.'

'In what context?'

'Like you're somebody he respects. Never mentions his wife or his son but he still talks about you.'

Fabian wondered if there wasn't a trace of resentment in Briant's voice.

'You caught him. Seems that entitles you to be held in the highest esteem.'

Fabian rarely thought of the people he imprisoned. It was something he'd trained himself to do. You had to move on and trust in the next cog of the justice mechanism. But he had thought about Christopher Wisher. He'd never had to deal with a psychopath like him and hoped he wouldn't have to again. But the notion that his name was on the killer's lips deeply unsettled him. There had to be a lot of criminals who wished him harm, many who had probably promised themselves to look him up when they got out, but the idea that Wisher spoke of him in a deferential way seemed much more alarming. 'Maybe he wants to lay the guilt on me now.' He stood and brandished the book.

'It's not exactly a page-turner. Perhaps you'll give me your thoughts when you have time?'

Fabian guessed Briant was still covering himself. 'Be glad to. But it's not priority.'

Briant briefly registered relief. 'Well, I'm sure you're eager to get back.' He got to his feet.

Fabian didn't feel like helping Briant wrap things up so easily. 'If there is anything in here that I need to double check…'

'You can speak to me direct,' the governor answered a little too quickly, his expression suddenly stern.

'Thank you.' He regarded Briant's stiff posture. 'There's nothing you want to tell me about in advance?'

He extended his palm. 'I'm sure you'll be mindful of Wisher's situation when you read it.'

It sounded more like a demand to Fabian. 'Thanks for the chat. I'll be in touch if I need to be.' He felt nearly as averse to shaking hands with Briant as he had with Wisher. Fabian did so, however, made eye contact, turned and left.

CHAPTER FIVE

Fabian pulled the door of his Audi shut. Even though it was heavy with damp he could still smell the prison on his dark green topcoat. The clouds had darkened considerably since he'd arrived. He didn't immediately drive away but watched the late afternoon rain spritzing the windscreen and turning the lights from the windows of Kerslake Prison into yellow stars. He knew Wisher's cell was in the east wing of the building. Was he looking out from it at him now?

The notebook felt heavy on his lap. The blue jacket told him it was a '2015 Desk Diary' and there were several crude lines of pen through the gold lettering. Was Briant nervous about him finding something inside? Like he said, however, he could have confiscated the book. Maybe that was why Wisher had wanted to put it in his hands personally. Despite Fabian's name scribbled at the bottom of the cover he ignored the urge to open it and dropped it onto the passenger seat. He was just pulling his belt across him when his phone rang. He took it out of his coat pocket.

It was Detective Sergeant Natasha Banner. 'Am I interrupting?'
'Just leaving.'
'That was quick.' She sounded surprised. 'What happened?'
'Very little.'
'What about the statement?'
'There wasn't one. He just wanted to give me a diary.'
'What's in it?'
'His priceless thoughts. I'll read it later.'

There was a pause. She knew he wouldn't leave the pages unopened for long. 'I'm finishing up a report. Why not bring it in and we'll both go over it.'

'Thanks but I want us to remain focussed on Maria Apostol.' It was her murder case that visiting Wisher had interrupted.

'OK…' She didn't sound convinced.

'Wisher's just going to have to get used to the idea that there's nothing ahead of him now except his sentence. Has Finch spoken to the other homeless people at the shelter?'

'He should be interviewing them now.'

'OK, I'm heading home but we'll have an early briefing tomorrow prior to my meeting with Metcalfe.'

'Eight?'

'Sounds about right.'

'I'll make sure everyone knows. If you need to speak to me later…'

'Thanks. I'll see you in the morning.' Fabian rang off and slid his car key into the ignition. But then he lifted his hand away. His gaze slid to the diary in the seat next to him and then returned to the rows of illuminated windows before him.

He started the engine and pulled out.

CHAPTER SIX

Despite it being a Monday evening, when he got home to his first floor maisonette, Fabian fixed himself a Gibson martini and seated himself on the leather couch in his compact lounge with the diary on his lap. He took a large gulp of the gin, put it on the coffee table and opened the front cover.

1st January was a blank page. He turned to the next and found that was too. The third was the same. He flicked through and found the first entry on October 22nd.

> *My punishment begins with something of an anti-climax.*
> *Prison offers no drama, just the gift of difficult days ahead.*

Today was the same date Wisher had started his sentence in 2015. Was this how he saw fit to mark his third anniversary of incarceration? Did he want to present his journal of prison life and, if so, why had he only given Fabian the first couple of months?

October 23rd
Restless and wary.

Wisher had written the same three words for the 24th, 25th and 26th. On the 27th he'd written:

> *Dead starling an omen. Suicide in cell 29 this evening.*

October 28th
Restless and wary. And full of dread.
October 29th
Martin. Dead face numbs me. Powerless. Sickened. No fingers can point at me any more.
October 30th
Sickening, debilitating realisation.
October 31st
Wings clipped.

November 1st and 2nd had the same entry:

Inertia.

Then:

November 3rd
No real tears yet. I'm going to be moved tomorrow though. Have to trust them.
November 4th
Bird in a cage. Can't escape. But listen. What's a little purgatory between friends?

November 5th to the 11th had the same entry:

Numb.

November 12th read:

Waiting. Anticipating. Sisyphean sentence continues…

Then the entries finished, nothing for the rest of the month or December. Why?

Fabian closed the diary. What was he doing? Allowing Wisher to draw him back in? Whatever he wanted to achieve with this record of his sentence, he wouldn't be a willing part of it. Particularly as he had no lead on the murderer of Maria Apostol, the Czech immigrant who had been stabbed repeatedly in a homeless shelter in Stockwell.

Wisher was locked away and would remain so. Maybe Briant had had something to hide but it would have to wait. He would review the diary with Banner when they had less pressing demands on their time.

But was he saying that because he was exhausted and needed an early night or because he suspected that Wisher was trying to manipulate him? He would probably be channelling Fabian now, imagining him poring over his words and taking great satisfaction from it.

Fabian slung the diary onto the coffee table and thoughtfully twisted the stem of his martini glass. He gulped it back and felt the burn, popped the onion left in the glass into his mouth and rose to head for the kitchen. Cooking then bed.

He'd preserved a number of duck legs in jars but extracting the confit from the goose fat and frying would only take minutes and he needed to start from scratch with something. Divert his thoughts for an hour before the food made him drowsy.

He'd run into a familiar blank wall with Maria Apostol and he knew decluttering his head and then getting some quality sleep would help him see the maze from above.

He assembled what fresh ingredients he had in the fridge and elected to make a frittata with eggs, potatoes, leftover Jambon de Savoie, fresh rosemary and lemon thyme. There was half a bottle of sauvignon blanc in the door of the fridge and he no longer bothered to tell himself he would have only one glass.

Wisher could lie in his cell believing whatever he wanted about what was happening outside of it.

Fabian took a bowl down from the shelf and cracked four eggs into it.

CHAPTER SEVEN

'How was your date?' Detective Constable Finch enquired as he adjusted the department's only portable heater. His powder blue shirt looked to be a size too small for his hefty frame and his usually just-out-of-bed hair had been flattened by the drizzle.

Fabian thudded a coffee onto his desk in the open plan office at Horseferry Police Station and prised off the lid. 'Brief. I think Wisher might need to go on a creative writing course, though.'

Natasha Banner swivelled around from her desk. 'Essential bedtime reading?' The thirty-eight-year-old Sri Lankan Detective Sergeant pushed her purple specs further up her nose.

'Didn't take me long. Less than a month of diary entries. One of them was about a suicide.'

Banner swivelled back and forth on the points of her heels. 'Kerslake *has* got a very high suicide rate.'

Fabian nodded grimly. 'The governor was at pains to tell me that Wisher was generous with his imagination.'

She raised an eyebrow. 'And was he?'

'All very cryptic. But I really don't know why Wisher wanted me to have the diary. Maybe he was just trying to get himself onto the programme at Bicknell Psychiatric. He's been turned down but perhaps he thinks I can make a recommendation.'

Banner pursed her lips. 'Did he ask you to?'

'Not directly. But he's manipulative. Maybe he's hoping that's the eventual outcome.'

'Who committed suicide?' Detective Sergeant McMann leaned back in his chair and chewed his pen. He'd obviously got caught in the storm on his bike ride in as his auburn hair and beard looked pretty bedraggled.

'He didn't say. October 27th. Claims a dead starling was an omen.'

'Still obsessed with dead birds?' Finch sat down at his desk.

'Birds?' McMann looked puzzled. He was the only team member who hadn't worked the Wisher case. He was thirty-two, a year younger than Finch and the newest addition to the team.

'It was a detail that was never released. The DCI at the time didn't want to encourage copycats,' Banner explained. 'Wisher used to leave a dead bird near the bodies wherever he dumped them. Always with its neck broken. Common varieties – blackbirds, sparrows…'

McMann shook his head. 'Why?'

Fabian shrugged. 'He never explained. Told us every minuscule detail of what he did to his victims but would never discuss the birds.' He turned to Finch. 'How did it go last night?'

'Couple of the guys down at the shelter gave the same description of the suspect on the CCTV. Said he occasionally turns up and offers casual labour.'

'No name?'

Finch shook his head. 'One of them said he's Czech.'

'Somebody there going to alert you next time he turns up?'

Finch nodded at Fabian.

Banner took off her specs to clean them. 'Maybe this guy is doing the circuit and we should be talking to all the shelters in the immediate area.'

Fabian took a sip of his coffee and nearly burned his lips. 'If he's scouting cheap labour for the Dvorak family perhaps he takes care of other business for them as well.'

McMann took his pen out of his mouth. 'Like disposing of people who object to being enslaved?'

He blew on the liquid. 'The Dvoraks use ex-soldiers to traffic people and his tattoos suggest they're military.'

'They're not clear enough in the image.' Banner nodded to the blow-up of his arm on the notice board. 'One of them is a pair of wings but it's impossible to make out the rest.'

McMann squinted at it. 'I'm sure it's a badge.'

But even magnified Fabian couldn't make it out. 'None of the people at the shelter remember them?'

'Apparently not,' Finch answered dubiously. 'There's a lot of spice being passed around there, though. Some of them don't even know what time of the day it is.'

'Go back to them if you come up empty-handed at the other shelters.'

Finch stood. 'Can do but I'd be surprised to find the same witnesses there.' He slid on his coat. 'There're people in and out of that place every day. Anything else?'

Fabian studied the image. 'We know Maria Apostol only stayed a couple of nights at St Vincent's shelter a week before her death. We have to establish where she was prior to that. We still haven't found one person who knew her. One friend who shared her predicament.'

'Maybe she was all alone,' Banner said, solemnly.

Fabian doubted that. 'She would probably have been part of a group. From what we've learned from escapees the Dvoraks scoop people up and condition them at one site before they're dispersed to brothels and other locations.'

'But with a police inquiry underway it's likely that's happened already.' Finch zipped up his coat. 'I'll keep putting her face under people's noses but there's a lot of fear about what happened to her. Very few people are going to want to endanger themselves, even if they *do* know who this guy is.'

'I'll see if I can pinpoint the tattoo and if it's for a specific military division.' McMann straightened at his keyboard.

'Check the files for the raid on Lime Street warehouse in 2017. Some of the Dvoraks' men were arrested then so see if you can find any matches.' Fabian turned to Banner. 'Everything OK at home?'

The other occupants of the office were poised on the edges of their tasks but hesitated to hear her reply. Banner looked uncomfortable and Fabian realised she hadn't shared her situation.

'Fine,' she answered definitively.

Fabian opened his mouth to apologise but thought better of it. That would confirm to the others she was dealing with something serious and she clearly wanted it to remain private. He felt everyone's gaze on him.

'Have to renew my pass.' Banner walked briskly out of the office.

Fabian chided himself for putting Banner in a situation where she would have to talk about her personal life. He wondered if she would even have told *him* if her appointments at Greenacre Hospital hadn't meant she had to juggle her hours. She hadn't divulged anything more than that. Fabian didn't know if it was her teenage son, her older husband or even her own health that was a concern.

'Everything OK?' McMann asked.

Finch was standing frozen waiting for the answer.

Fabian didn't know how to respond. *All fine? Cut her some slack?* She wouldn't be happy with either of those. 'She'll tell you if she needs to.'

Neither of them seemed satisfied with that.

'Back to work.'

Finch headed out and McMann returned his attention to the computer screen.

He would have a word with Banner in private. Let her offer up any details if she chose to. He wouldn't push. He knew she'd probably rather divert herself with work.

He glanced at his watch. Fabian still had a few minutes before his meeting with DCI Metcalfe and decided to check out a date.

The 27th October 2015. Who in cell 29 of Kerslake Prison had chosen that day to commit suicide?

But he couldn't find anything online. The last record of a suicide at Kerslake was April 2018. Prisoner named Howard Warbeck. Was Briant right about Wisher taking liberties with reality or was something at the prison being concealed? Fabian decided that, when he had more time, he would call the governor for another chat.

CHAPTER EIGHT

At first Fabian thought he'd misheard the noise. It sounded like a single light knock on his door but he couldn't remember the last person who had come up to the entrance of his first floor maisonette. He always picked up his mail from the mat in the downstairs porch and nobody really had cause to climb the stairs except him.

That's why he initially ignored the sound. He thought it might have been activity in the downstairs flat. His curiosity got the better of him, however. Fabian ceased finely shaving a garlic clove, put down his knife on the chopping board and walked from the back kitchen to the front door and opened it. Nobody outside. He was just about to close it again when he caught sight of a dark shape on the faded saffron carpet.

It was a dead bird.

Fabian's attention shot to the small window over the stairs. The tiny pane at the top was open as it always was. Could the bird have flown straight through it? But he could already feel the slow bubbles of dread beginning to rise inside him.

He lightly nudged the bird with the toe of his shoe. Its head lolled as if its neck were broken. There was no movement. No twitches. He knew of birds flying into windowpanes and stunning themselves but why would it have flown at a solid door? He bent to his knees but something stopped him from touching it further.

It was a starling. Fabian immediately recalled Wisher's entry about it being an omen.

He carefully stepped over the bird and quickly descended the stairs to the hallway. He pushed the glass door at the bottom and dashed to the porch. The door was on the latch. Tugging it he made his way along the path to the gate. The metal handle was locked in place but he snapped the metal and swung it wide.

It was early evening but there was nobody in the street. Fabian could see his old marital home was in darkness. Harriet was obviously out and, despite his reminders, had forgotten to leave a lamp on.

He knew the road had no CCTV. He'd briefly considered getting a video intercom for visitors but had dispensed with the idea when he realised that he very rarely received any. Fabian walked back into the house and closed the front door behind him, locking it.

Pausing at the end of the hall he listened at the front door of the downstairs flat. Murmuring from within. Should he disturb them? He knocked.

No reply.

Fabian rapped again. The voices stopped and the door opened. It was Dina, one half of the couple who had lived there since 2016. Normally blonde and immaculate, she'd allowed her roots to grow out and looked like she hadn't washed her hair for some time. Her brown sockets told Fabian she hadn't slept.

'Apologies for disturbing you…'

She shook her head and seemed dazed.

'You left the front door on the latch.'

Dina's face wrinkled in apology. 'I'm sorry. Mike was unloading shopping and must have forgotten.'

'Easily done.' They'd had words about it before. He didn't want to make it any easier for burglars to gain entry to the flats. 'I just wondered if you heard anybody else out here in the past few moments.'

The tall, shaven-headed Mike appeared behind Dina. 'Hi, Tom.'

Dina turned to him. 'You left the door on the latch again.'

'Sorry.' But Mike didn't look it. He always reacted to Tom's polite requests for them to lock it as if he was overreacting.

'Did you see anyone else out there when you were bringing in the groceries?' she asked him.

'No.' He shook his head once. 'Why?'

Fabian didn't want to alarm them. 'Just thought I heard someone down here.'

Dina looked worried.

'Was probably us,' Mike reassured him.

'How long have you both been in?'

Mike looked at his watch. 'About half an hour.'

So the door had been unlocked all that time. 'Nobody hanging around when you unloaded?'

'Not that I noticed.' Mike seemed eager to close the door.

'Why so concerned?' Dina had guessed there was more to it than just him hearing a noise.

'Think we should keep it locked.'

'Will do,' Mike said quickly.

He knew Mike thought he was a pain. There had always been awkwardness between them ever since he'd had to knock on the door when they'd held their house-warming party and it had gone on until three in the morning. He'd waited, let them have their fun but the music had just got louder and louder. Fabian had been trying to catch up on sleep but thought he'd been reasonable about it when he'd courteously asked him to turn it down. Mike always spoke to him when they bumped into each other but his greetings always seemed sarcastic. Dina did her best to defuse it whenever the three of them spoke. A cooking smell wafted out at Fabian. 'OK, don't want to disturb your dinner.'

'Thanks.' Mike started closing the door.

Dina mouthed 'sorry' again as it shut.

Fabian climbed the stairs to his flat and looked down at the dead bird. It was too much of a coincidence that it would end up outside his door only a few days after reading about it in Wisher's diary. He'd been uneasy since he'd sat down with it after his visit to Kerslake.

Dead starling an omen. Suicide in cell 29 this evening.

The bird's dark eyes were still clear. It had died recently. But how recently? Fabian got his phone and took several pictures of it. The he went to the kitchen and fetched a zip freezer bag and used a pair of plastic tongs to delicately pick up the animal and slide its carcass inside.

'OK.' He held it up and examined its limp form. 'Let's keep you nice and fresh.' He cleared some space in the bottom of the fridge and put the starling inside. Fabian closed the door.

It was October 27th. Someone had had ample opportunity to get into the house and leave it on his doormat. Was this part of Wisher's game? Did he have people on the outside willing to do something like this on his behalf? Sounded like he had a number of visitors at Kerslake, followers who hero-worshipped his crimes. Maybe Wisher had decided to punish him.

Why now? Had his resentment built up over the years? Fabian was determined not to allow him back under his skin. But he'd take the bird to the lab first thing.

CHAPTER NINE

There was a suspended atmosphere in the office when Fabian got in the following morning. He dumped his leather case containing the starling on the desk and was about to open it when he met Banner's stern expression. 'What is it?'

'Wisher's dead.' She waited for his reaction.

The news seemed more puzzling than shocking to him. 'How?'

'Suicide.' Banner indicated her screen. 'It's all over social media. Hanged himself in his cell last night.'

But Fabian didn't feel the relief he should have. He met Finch's gaze.

'Couldn't have happened to a nicer guy,' Finch said, deadpan.

'So, his little meeting with you was a goodbye.' But Banner didn't seem convinced.

Finch folded his meaty arms. 'Why now?'

'Maybe because the opportunity arose.' Fabian pointed at Banner's screen. 'Any details on how he did it?'

She shook her head.

'Perhaps he realised if he wasn't going to get his comfy cell in Bicknell things weren't going to get any easier,' McMann suggested.

Fabian nodded. He knew the news would be stirring up some disturbing memories for Banner and Finch as well.

Banner opened her Twitter feed. 'He's trending.'

Fabian sat down and eyed his leather case. He remembered what Wisher had said to him when he'd left.

Take care, Tom.

Was that farewell or a threat? Had he already made his mind up about killing himself then?

'His bio on Wiki has already been updated.' McMann shook his head in disbelief.

'What a relief to taxpayers. Would have preferred him to rot, though.' Banner strode over to the coffee machine.

But Fabian knew she wouldn't be able to shake him off easily either. 'Remember our conversation about dead birds?' He didn't wait for a response. Just opened his case; took out the bagged starling and placed it on the desk.

Finch rose. 'Where did you get that?'

'I found it on my doorstep last night.'

'Shit muffins.' He circled around Fabian's desk.

Banner's eyes lifted from the animal and met his. She'd already made the connection he had.

'Wisher's omen.' Fabian confirmed. 'He wrote about seeing this before the suicide in cell 29.'

Finch examined it closely. 'You think one of his disciples planted it there?'

'They know where you live?' McMann seemed alarmed.

'Looks that way.' Fabian took the diary out of the case and placed it beside the bird.

'They're trying to scare you.' Finch leaned closer to it. 'Neck broken?'

'Just like the others.' Fabian nudged the head through the polythene.

McMann contemplated the creature. 'Some sicko's idea of fun?'

'Hell of a price to pay.' Fabian opened the diary. But being stalked at home wasn't his primary concern. 'Killing yourself to prove an omen true.'

'What time did the bird turn up?' Banner returned without a coffee.

'Someone knocked my door at eight.'

Her expression hardened. 'Wisher died around that time last night. I think we can safely forget about this being a coincidence.'

CHAPTER TEN

'Is this going to take long? I have a lot to deal with since last night's… episode.' Briant's voice sounded strained.

Fabian closed the door of the mini glass conference room and sat on the edge of the desk with his mobile tight to his ear. 'I was wondering if you'd be able to give me a few more specifics.'

The governor of Kerslake sighed. 'He's no longer your problem. Just a series of cluster headaches for me. Now, if you'll excuse me…'

'Of course. Maybe we can discuss some of Wisher's diary entries when it's convenient.' Fabian waited.

There was a brief pause before Briant answered. 'What do you need to know?'

'You're busy now. Maybe I can make an appointment to talk to you when you have more time.' But Fabian guessed Briant wouldn't want him at the prison.

'*If* I have time.' He sounded suspicious. 'What are you not telling me?'

'I just wondered if you'd be able to tell me who died in cell 29?'

'Is this a joke?'

'No. Wisher mentions a dead starling being an omen before a suicide in cell 29.'

'Wisher was in cell 29.' Briant sounded exasperated.

Fabian was briefly speechless.

'I warned you not to take anything in those pages seriously.'

Fabian felt unease start to effervesce again. 'Maybe we should. How long was he in cell 29?'

'Since he arrived at Kerslake.'

'And did what he wrote in the diary not alarm you?'

'Why would it? It was a journal for 2015. He very clearly didn't commit suicide in his cell then.'

'But he has now. And it's the same date as in the diary. Twenty-seventh of October.'

Briant breathed on the mouthpiece for a few seconds. 'And what does he say on the 28th?'

Fabian looked down at the book on the desk. '" *Restless and wary. And full of dread.*"'

'You've read the other entries?'

'Yes.'

'Then you have to see they were nothing more than fragmented thoughts. I can assure you they bear no resemblance to his days at Kerslake.'

But Fabian was beginning to realise what they might refer to. 'A dead starling turned up on my doorstep last night.'

'What?'

'Can you give me the details of anyone who has been to visit Wisher?'

'Across three years?'

'I'd like their names.'

'OK. I can access those for you. You think Wisher is using somebody to target you?'

'It's highly likely. Though why he would take his own life now is baffling.'

'Wisher was ill,' Briant stated simply.

'How ill?'

'Brain cancer.'

'Why the hell didn't you tell me that?'

'He requested the diagnosis remain private. Obviously now discretion isn't an issue.'

'Didn't you think it would have had a bearing on my meeting with him?'

'It's why I've never given any credence to what he wrote. I knew his mental health was steadily degenerating.'

'When was he diagnosed?'

'Tail end of 2017.'

'Did his family know?'

'I don't think so. There's been no contact between them since he was convicted.'

'So how did he kill himself?'

Briant sighed. 'A plastic carpet tie. He secured it around his neck and the post of his bunk.'

'How d'you think he managed to get hold of it?'

Briant paused. 'We had the north admin wing decorated in September. Tools went missing. If Wisher wanted to get hold of it he could have.'

'I didn't get the impression he socialised with the other inmates.'

'No. But he used the exercise yard.'

'Could he have been given it by one of his visitors?'

'Security procedures during visiting are rigorous,' Briant said, as if quoting from a manual.

'But fallible.'

'He would have been searched before and after.'

'He could have easily concealed a strip of plastic.'

'No. It wouldn't have come from outside.'

Fabian could hear the tremor of panic in the governor's voice. A prisoner had died on Briant's watch and if what Banner had said about Kerslake's record was true it wasn't the first time. 'I'd still like to see the list of visitors. If someone is dropping gifts off for me I'd like to know who it is.'

'Of course. I'll get onto that.'

'Anything else you think's relevant?'

'Not that I can think of. He was found in his cell last night. There was no untoward behaviour beforehand.'

'And he didn't leave a note?'

Again Briant briefly paused. 'Nothing.'

But he suspected that Wisher had already written the message he wanted to leave behind long in advance of his suicide and had already handed it to Fabian.

CHAPTER ELEVEN

Fabian looked again at the cover of Wisher's diary where his name had been scrawled and then turned the pages and re-examined the first entry.

October 22nd
My punishment begins with something of an anti-climax.
Prison offers no drama, just the gift of difficult days ahead.

It wasn't Wisher's diary. The year 2015 had been scribbled out on the cover. Fabian's name was at the bottom. This was an entry that Wisher had written for him. He'd thought it referred to the beginning of Wisher's sentence but reading it now he saw that it could easily describe his trip to the prison when he'd seen Wisher for the last time. The diary was the gift. Was it actually Fabian's punishment that was beginning?

He studied the pages that followed.

October 23rd
Restless and wary.

That was an accurate description of how he'd felt after his visit. The entry was the same for the 24th, 25th and 26th. Then:

October 27th
Dead starling an omen. Suicide in cell 29 this evening.

And the next day said:

October 28th
Restless and wary. And full of dread.

Fabian turned the page.

October 29th
Martin. Dead face numbs me. Powerless. Sickened. No fingers can point at me any more.

Martin Prentice was the name of Wisher's second victim. Or was Martin the person who had agreed to carry out Wisher's instructions? Had he laid the starling at his door and what else would he be prepared to do?

October 30th
Sickening, debilitating realisation.

Fabian felt the dread solidify inside him. Wisher was right. Fabian dialled Briant again. 'I'm going to need that list right now.'

'I have other priorities.'

'I want the names. I really don't believe Wisher was suffering from his condition when he wrote the diary.'

'Why not?'

'In fact, I think he was more than in charge of his faculties. More so than when he meticulously planned to murder each of his victims.'

'How on earth do you come to that conclusion?' Briant scoffed.

'The starling, the suicide in 29 on the exact date. I think he's written the diary for me. And he's telling me exactly what's going to happen in the future. It began the day he handed it to me. And I think tomorrow somebody could be murdered.'

CHAPTER TWELVE

Fabian's team were silent as he relayed the conversation he'd just had with Briant.

'So this is *your* diary.' Banner was sitting on her desk, leafing through it.

'"October 29th. *Martin. Dead face numbs me. Powerless. Sickened. No fingers can point at me any more.*"' Fabian indicated the entry. 'When I first read it I thought that was a reference to Martin Prentice.'

Finch gulped down a whole paper cone of water. 'Who can forget Martin Prentice?'

'Wisher's second victim?' McMann remembered.

Even though McMann hadn't been on the case Fabian knew that anyone who had watched Angelina Friedmann's documentary about the investigation wouldn't forget Prentice. He'd been attacked in Richmond Park in broad daylight and Wisher's mutilation of his body had been extensive. 'He was one of eight victims attacked in the day. Almost like Wisher was trying to get caught.'

'Did he ever confirm that was his intention?' McMann crossed the office to Banner's desk.

'No,' Banner replied. '"*Dead face numbs me*"? The twenty-ninth is tomorrow.'

Fabian nodded gravely.

McMann peered over her shoulder. 'But there's a big difference between leaving dead animals on a doorstep and actually committing murder. D'you really think one of Wisher's followers would go that far?'

'There are a lot of wannabe psychos out there.' Finch sighed.

'And there's already been one alleged copycat killing,' Banner reminded them.

'When?' McMann asked.

'Alleged.' Fabian repeated. 'Brompton Cemetery. A rent boy, Rodney Trent, was found raped and murdered there three months after Wisher started his sentence. There was a dead blackbird near the body. It was believed to be a coincidence.'

McMann frowned. 'Didn't you say the dead birds were a detail never revealed to the public?'

Finch screwed up the cone and dumped it in the bin. 'Yeah, and the bird was already decomposing. Wisher's were usually fresh. Chances are it was rotting there already. Where's your starling now?'

'Down at the lab.' Fabian had taken it to forensics after his first phone conversation with Briant.

'And you didn't think there was a connection?' McMann asked.

Fabian hadn't been involved in the Brompton murder inquiry but had kept tabs on it. 'Wisher never had sex with his victims.'

'Although Trent's body *was* mutilated,' Banner added.

'There were no suspects?' McMann squinted at Wisher's scrawl.

'One. But there was insufficient evidence.' Fabian didn't have any problem recalling the name though. 'Sean Coles. He was a regular client of Trent's and the last man to be seen with him before his death. It was very likely him.'

'Said he hadn't even heard of Christopher Wisher. Which, after the media storm, was difficult to believe,' Banner said sceptically.

'We should definitely talk to him. But I'm more interested in getting that list of Wisher's visitors from Briant.' But Fabian wondered if he was jumping the gun.

'Should we take this to Metcalfe now?' Banner had had the same thought.

Because of the DCI's resentment towards Fabian involving the media in the Wisher investigation Fabian guessed he wouldn't want him stirring things back up again. 'I've no choice.'

Finch joined the group at the desk. 'Maybe this is just Wisher's last ditch attempt to mess with your head.'

'I hope it is. But if there's more to this than scare tactics I can't just sit on it. I want you all to keep focussed on Maria Apostol in the meantime, though. Still no joy at St Vincent's?'

Finch shook his head. 'Only one of the witnesses I interviewed originally was there last night. And he seemed very reluctant to talk.'

Fabian guessed as much. 'You think the Dvoraks might have been threatening people?'

'Possibly.' Finch exhaled. 'But Maria isn't the only casualty this month. Two people from the shelter were taken to hospital last night after a gang of hoodies attacked them. One died and the other has brain damage.'

'So Maria is yesterday's news already.' Fabian knew that was a depressing reality. 'What about the other shelters?'

'Same situation. And, even if they did, nobody wants to admit they knew Maria.'

'Any luck with the tattoo?'

McMann looked up from the diary. 'A lot of similar military designs but the magnified image we have is too low-resolution to get a match.'

'We need a better image. You've asked for the CCTV footage from the other shelters?'

Finch ran a palm through his mess of hair. 'Only one has a camera and that was busted, deliberately by the looks of it.'

'That might be significant. Which one?'

'Lingham Shelter in Camberwell.'

'Anyone familiar with the Dvoraks there?'

'Everyone knows the Dvoraks but nobody wants to talk about them.'

'What about the people who run it?'

'They're just as scared.'

'Keep pushing.'

'That's easier said than done. We don't offer any protection and they're vulnerable as soon as they talk to me.'

'D'you think the Dvoraks have some of the volunteers on the payroll?'

Finch nodded at Fabian. 'Without a doubt. Cherry-picking. As soon as they spot a likely candidate they're making the call.'

'So there's no safe place for these people?'

'It's why so many of them don't stay at the shelters.'

Fabian could tell how frustrated Finch was. He'd interviewed plenty of homeless people himself. Knew it was a fragile life they led and that helping to convict the predators who preyed on them was much less important than daily survival. 'You know how to talk to them.' It was Finch's skill but Fabian knew that would only get him so far.

'I'll go back to Lingham. But chances are they're going to be even less willing to speak to me than the last time.'

'What about this?' McMann indicated the diary in Banner's hands.

Fabian clenched his jaw. 'I'm going to talk to Metcalfe now.'

'Want some support?' Banner closed the book.

'I don't think he'd appreciate two against one.' Fabian held out his hand.

She passed it to him. 'Even *he's* got to realise you're the only one qualified to deal with this.'

'Precisely why he'll probably try to prise it from my hands.' He headed for the DCI's office.

CHAPTER THIRTEEN

'So, who's the first to know about this, me or Angelina Friedmann?'

'I've told you, I haven't been in touch with her since the end of Wisher's trial.' So far, Fabian's meeting with Metcalfe had been textbook.

'Of course, she's a news exec now. Extracted what she needed from you,' the bald and increasingly portly DCI said significantly then finished chewing a chunk of panini. He picked up the remainder from where it rested on a wax wrapper on his desk and eyed the diary that Fabian had opened in front of him. 'Any reason to believe this is anything more than Wisher playing mind games?'

'The dead bird outside my door.'

The DCI took another generous bite and spoke with his mouth full. 'I'm sure Wisher has plenty of fanatics willing to pull off a prank like that.'

'A prank?'

'Murder, though? That's your interpretation of what he's written.'

'You don't think this is worth taking seriously?'

'Of course. But I'd like you to leave it with me.'

It was nothing he hadn't anticipated, knew Metcalfe would use it as an opportunity to frustrate him. But Fabian closed the diary and barely restrained himself from snatching it up off the desk. 'It was me he gave it to.'

'And perhaps you should have come to me with it before you spoke to Briant.'

Was that the reason Metcalfe was being so spiky? 'You've made it crystal clear to me you want closure on the investigation.'

'And up until a few minutes ago I thought his suicide might guarantee that.'

'I didn't ask for my audience with him. You sent me to Kerslake.'

'You shouldn't have accepted anything from him.' Metcalfe swallowed noisily.

'I need to handle this. Wisher believes – believed – there was a connection between us.'

'Is there?'

'No.'

'Then you won't object to me allowing someone else to take charge. I don't want you getting fixated again.'

'Fixated? That's why I caught him in the first place.'

'You know what I'm talking about. Friedmann's documentary wasn't good for the department.'

'Because?'

'Wisher should have been caught sooner,' Metcalfe stated, unblinking.

Fabian was momentarily breathless. He fought his temper. 'Perhaps he would have if I'd been given the manpower I'd requested.'

Metcalfe waved his hand dismissively. 'You made the arrest. You interviewed Wisher. If he imagined there was a connection between the two of you—'

'That was how *he* read the situation. But he does – did believe that, and if this campaign is targeted at me then I'm the best equipped to deal with it.'

'We don't know if this *is* a campaign.'

'So are you willing to keep this in your pending tray until somebody's dead?'

Metcalfe ran his tongue around the morsels in his mouth and regarded Fabian with barely concealed contempt. 'No.'

'Maria Apostol is my priority. But I'd like your permission to compile a preliminary list of people we may need to talk to.'

'If?'

Fabian nodded at the diary. 'If there's anything in here that's more than a threat.'

Metcalfe chewed thoughtfully but Fabian doubted even he would be able justify handing it over to another officer. They would still have to come back to Fabian.

'October 29th is tomorrow.'

Fabian nodded.

'You've got one week after that date. If it proves to be nothing more than a joke on you, let it go.'

'OK.' For the first time Fabian hoped that Metcalfe's instincts were right.

Metcalfe picked up the diary and offered it to Fabian. He took hold of it but Metcalfe retained his grip for a few moments before letting it go.

It reminded him of Wisher doing something similar and how oblivious Fabian had been when he'd accepted it.

'One week. Now tell me what progress you're making with Maria Apostol.'

'Looks like the Dvoraks.'

'I could have told you that. Any closer to the guy on the CCTV footage?'

'People at the shelters are too scared to talk.'

'Let's knuckle down then,' Metcalfe said brusquely. 'Set our sights on a murder that has actually been committed.'

CHAPTER FOURTEEN

She would end it today. That was the single thought going around Nadine's head. She pumped her arms and felt the impact of her feet on the concrete path smart in her kneecaps. Whatever happened, whatever he said, she would end it today. The mini mantra overrode the Jack Savoretti song that was turned down low and rustling against her eardrums. Nadine didn't even register the cold rain driving at her.

She was nearing the idol in Battersea Park. The place it had all started. It seemed apt to finish it there as well. She could see him standing in front of it, waiting for her. His face lit up when he saw Nadine. Like it did every time. Her husband didn't do that any more.

He was eager for her. Looked unbelievably toned in his running gear. The sex was intense. So ardent. Maybe she would pay for a room in the nearby Metz Hotel one more time and then tell him afterwards…

No. She'd told herself that the last time and hadn't been able to do it. It would feel like she'd used and dispensed with him. She had to be the grown-up. Was the grown-up.

He's nineteen years younger than you, she reminded herself as she approached him. But that fact never failed to boost her. Her brain scrabbled for the dog-eared list of cons she'd been compiling over the weeks of their affair.

Kieran was an impoverished sports psychology student. She was a majority shareholder in her husband's crypto mining company.

Kieran was a millennial who seemed to think he was entitled to everything without working for it and she wanted to bash his head in for being so naïve. *Remember that. Remember that.*

But Kieran was sweet. Kieran hung on her every word. Kieran didn't close his eyes when he was coming. OK, that was a bit creepy but he clearly wasn't thinking of somebody else when they were having sex.

She screwed up the list of pros again and pulled out her earphones as she reached him.

'Hey there.' Kieran's eyes were wide as she approached but there was uncertainty lurking on his glistening face.

'Hey.' How was she going to broach this? Just speak from the heart or go for the way she'd rehearsed it?

'Ready to go?'

Usually he didn't wait for an answer, just headed off along the path and joked as she tried to keep up. There was a trace of anxiety in his gaze, however, and Nadine knew she had to seize on it. 'No. Not today.'

He didn't frown. Didn't seem surprised. 'I thought you sounded strange on the phone last night.'

Nadine felt the accumulated happiness of the past three months that had gathered in a bubble in the middle of her chest burst before she said what he was expecting to hear. 'You'll never know what our time together has meant to me.' She recited as she'd rehearsed but forgot what came next and felt the happiness suddenly drain out of her. She fought her emotions.

'It doesn't have to stop.' But Kieran's stolid expression knew it would.

'I don't want to make this any worse than it has to be.' Thank god, the words were coming back. 'It's so not you. And not me either. It's circumstances that are never going to work for us.' That was the part she was most proud of. Nadine saw his eyes blur. *Oh god, don't do that.*

He nodded. Knew she'd made her mind up.

He was intelligent, sensitive. If they'd met when she was his age… 'It's probably better we just run in opposite directions.' Her throat tightened. 'I'll use a different park now.'

He nodded again, his mouth clamped shut.

She leaned forward to kiss him but he'd already turned. She watched him go, his pace steady. Felt the empty space in her chest and released a sob. She hadn't thought it would be as painful.

But Nadine loved her life more than Kieran. Not her husband. That had never really worked and she shouldn't have been so eager to marry. But she adored her teenage daughters and the fact that she could afford to give them everything they wanted but didn't. And she certainly wasn't about to destroy what she'd built for them for the selfish sake of having the relationship she'd wished she'd had in her twenties. This feeling would pass. Kieran would find somebody else. Better it end now before her feelings wrought proper damage.

Everything had gone quiet and Nadine tried to plug herself back into her environment. It was after two on a Monday afternoon and the lunchtime runners had evaporated. Only a handful of onlookers would have seen the exchange and she focussed on the few people on the path. Having an affair with her trainer was a bit of a cliché but it at least allowed her to meet him in public.

This would come back on her, though. Perhaps she deserved that. Her legs felt wobbly and she walked to a bench and sat down. She could still see Kieran tracing the camber of the park.

Agonising as it was, she'd done the right thing. Take a deep breath, think of a time not far from now. Think of the girls. Think of the summer holidays she'd planned with them. She put her earphones back in and turned Jack up loud.

Kieran had almost disappeared when fingers grabbed the bun of hair on the top of her head and jerked it back. A hand was cupped over her mouth and she could smell something antiseptic.

I'm being mugged. Her thoughts yelled over Jack Savoretti.

The music drowned out the sound of her sob and then her neck was stinging cold. She put her hand to it and it was wet and hot.

Nadine tried to cry out but Kieran had already disappeared from sight.

CHAPTER FIFTEEN

As Fabian skirted the trees bordering the edge of the path in Battersea Park, he knew exactly what he was about to find. Mills, the potbellied pathologist, was already there, his white suit and those of the three techs he was monitoring glowing in the dwindling afternoon light. A handful of other uniformed officers were dotted about the area. The track had been closed off to the public and was eerily empty. Fabian blinked against a draught of cold drizzle. The Thames beyond looked dirty brown under the dingy sky.

He and Banner stepped over the short red fence and crossed the grass to where yellow police tape delineated the piece of land that had now taken on a terrible new significance. Mills turned and met his eye as he approached.

'I'm getting déjà vu,' Banner said bleakly.

All three of them had worked the Wisher case and the pathologist's grim expression was identical to the nine occasions they'd shared those previous murder scenes.

'Someone's idea of a memorial?' Mills looked pale and drawn and placed his hand in its customary place, his knuckles resting against the base of his spine.

Fabian knew that Mills' lumbago would soon bring him the retirement that he was always talking about but seemed reluctant to embrace.

Mills winced. 'Step behind me.'

They followed him to where the victim lay on her back, both arms extended above her head.

Fabian felt the blood drain through his feet. It was exactly the way Wisher used to arrange the bodies. 'ID?'

'None on her. We've got her phone though so we should hear from somebody soon.'

'And no witnesses.' But Fabian already knew the answer.

'Just like old times.' Mills itched his bald pate with the back of his blue-gloved hand.

The woman's eyes were closed as if she were concentrating on the music in her earphones. She looked to be in her forties, her features silver white and contrasting with the maroon scarf of dried blood about her throat. Fabian could see the depth of the laceration through her Adam's apple and the dark band above the elasticated waist of her powder blue sweatshirt. There was a bulk bulging beneath it.

Banner swallowed. 'Same mutilation?'

Mills nodded. 'Incision to the belly. Put their hand inside her and rummaged around.'

Wisher had done it to all of his victims and he'd never been drawn on his reasons under interrogation. Fabian's eyes flitted about the scene and fell on a dark shape to the right of the body.

Mills followed his gaze. 'House martin. Not a very common bird.'

Banner stepped closer to examine the tiny creature.

Fabian could see its head was crudely twisted.

'Fresh like the others,' Mills told Banner.

Fabian had wondered if the Martin referred to in the diary entry was a reference to Wisher's second victim or the intended victim's name. The serial killer had left a variety of birds near the victims but never a house martin. Then he noticed the blood in the palms of the dead woman's hands. They were curled into claws but he could see that all the fingertips of both had been cut off.

'That's something new.' Mills painfully knelt beside the woman. 'He never used to take digits.'

Martin. Dead face numbs me. Powerless. Sickened. No fingers can point at me any more.

'Whoever did this adhered painstakingly to the diary entry.' Fabian gazed through the trees to the small crowd chatting to one of the uniformed officers further down the path.

'Not even Metcalfe could dispute that.' Banner stepped carefully back to the body.

'Diary?'

'Fill him in,' Fabian said to Banner without taking his eyes from the faces around the uniformed officer. He scanned them, looked for a different expression to the others. Someone who didn't share the curiosity around him. But he couldn't pick out anyone whose features betrayed them.

'Sir?'

Fabian was aware he'd zoned everything else out and turned back to Banner.

'Back to the diary, examine every entry?'

Fabian already had. 'The next significant one is in two days' time.'

'Two days?' Mills hissed out air. 'And your prime suspect is dead.'

'Let me know as soon as you've identified her. Report by tomorrow?'

Mills nodded at Fabian. 'It's like he was here himself.' He regarded the body thoughtfully.

Banner folded her arms tight to herself. 'So every death has been laid out for us.'

Fabian returned his attention to the crowd with the officer and the truth of that was suddenly heavy in his stomach. 'And we have pages to go.' He recalled what the entry for the following day had said. He'd thought it had been Wisher's reaction to the beginning of his suffering but it was actually a declaration of his own.

Sickening, debilitating realisation.

CHAPTER SIXTEEN

Three hours after an emergency briefing with Metcalfe, the Maria Apostol case had been handed over to DI Nettles and Fabian had been ordered to direct all his resources at the Wisher copycat.

Just before eight that evening, he rapped on the white Masonite door to a council semi in Parsons Green and addressed the person who answered it. 'Mrs Naylor?' Fabian knew Bruce still lived with his parents.

The fifty-something woman with bowl cut grey hair was wearing a faded yellow tracksuit that hung off her skinny build and had a vape cigarette in her hand.

'I'm Detective Inspector Fabian and this is Detective Sergeant Banner. We're here to speak to Bruce.' The aroma of sickly sweet berries wafted out at him and he fought back a cough.

'Yes. He said you were going to call in.' She stepped back to allow them to enter.

Fabian thought she seemed more excited than concerned about her son's potential incrimination. 'Thank you.' He entered the hallway with Banner close behind.

Mrs Naylor closed the front door. 'He's upstairs in his office. Ainsley!'

'Send them up!' An irritated voice replied.

Fabian exchanged a frown with Banner and Mrs Naylor caught it.

'Bruce is his blog name,' she explained.

'Right.' Banner nodded uncertainly at her.

'Tells me you're consulting with him.' Mrs Naylor seemed proud of that.

'Something like that.' Fabian put his foot on the bottom stair.

'Can I get you a cup of tea?'

'Fuck's sake, Ma! Just send them up!'

Mrs Naylor shrugged her shoulders and smirked, as if they all somehow found the outburst lovable.

They climbed the stairs and walked into the room ahead with its door ajar and light on.

The office was a bedroom with a desk in it. Fabian absorbed the plastic seven-day multi-pill dispenser on the bedside table, a panoply of other medication canisters behind it.

Ainsley Naylor was sitting in a swivel chair at the desk wearing an earphone and mic. His head squatted into his shoulders so his tight curly black fronds of hair lay to the edges of his shoulders. His fingers rested linked on his barrel chest and their tips were orange. 'Sorry about her.'

'Because?'

Naylor seemed puzzled by Fabian's response. 'Onset of Alzheimer's or something.'

Fabian was staggered that Naylor was in his late twenties. His whole demeanour was that of a surly teenager. His room was characterless, however. No posters or other adornments. The mushroom walls were quite blank.

'Hang on. Have to go, guys.' Naylor turned to his Xbox and logged out of whatever game he was in the middle of.

Fabian noted the three-litre bottle of Sprite and huge bag of Cheetos beside it. Explained the orange fingers.

Naylor swivelled back to them, his thick dark eyebrows raised.

'Want to take that off.' Banner said with her best schoolmistress tone and indicated the headset.

Naylor sighed nasally and dropped it into his lap.

Fabian had gathered that he probably ran the household and wasn't used to obeying instructions. He was nine years older than Tilly. She'd never been allowed to act like this. That had been more down to Harriet than him. He'd had the easy ride because of his job and she'd always been the disciplinarian. It had been the touch-paper for a lot of heated arguments over the years. 'I understand you visited Christopher Wisher last week.'

Naylor smirked, obviously pleased it now made him the centre of attention.

'Why?' Fabian simply asked.

He frowned a little too deeply. 'To shoot the breeze.'

Fabian acknowledged it was the term Wisher used. 'Why did you start visiting him?'

'Because it was Christopher Wisher,' Naylor retorted in a 'duh' kind of way.

'And you know who I am.'

'Of course. Chris never spoke about you like you were his nemesis or anything, though.'

'Chris?' Banner aped.

Naylor nodded but didn't shift his focus from Fabian. 'I thought you were taller.'

'I never fail to disappoint. How long have you been going to see him?'

Naylor squinted as if he was struggling to remember. 'Since April 12th last year.'

Fabian could tell it wasn't a struggle, though. 'And how many times since then?'

'Eight.'

'So, you've been interviewing him for your blog?'

'Never thought he'd agree so when he did I couldn't believe it.'

'What did you discuss with him?'

He smirked again. 'The transcripts are on the blog.'

'We've seen it.'

Naylor grinned, visibly pleased that Fabian had been looking at his page. 'Hope you clicked on a few sponsors.'

'Any chats off mic?'

'Plenty.' Naylor was clearly enjoying baiting him.

'Did he talk about suicide?'

'He talked about a lot of things.'

Fabian hardened his tone. 'Did he discuss suicide?'

Naylor shook his head.

'And did he tell you he was ill?' Banner pressed.

He turned to her. 'Yes.'

But Fabian could tell it was news to him. 'So, he didn't tell you everything.'

He returned his attention to Fabian. 'Why are you so interested in my relationship with him?'

'You were one of four regular visitors Wisher had. Do you know any of the others?'

'I know Jennifer Keene.'

She was next on Fabian's list. 'You've met?'

'No. I just know *of* her.'

'How?' He could see enmity flash in Naylor's eyes.

'How could I not? She's like a rash on the Internet. And I know she's trolled me more than a few times.'

'Why?'

'She acts like she's got the global rights to Chris. Claimed she'd had sex with him but I know she didn't.'

'Why would she say that?' Fabian was looking forward to that conversation.

'Because she's deranged.' Naylor fidgeted with the headset in his lap. 'Chris thought she was a crackpot.'

Banner checked the notes on her phone. 'But she's been a regular visitor.'

'Yes. I think Chris was… entertained by her.'

'You didn't feel jealous then?' Fabian continued and studied his reaction.

Theatrical mortification tugged his features. 'No.'

'What was the last thing you discussed with him?'

He shrugged briefly and his shoulders remained raised. 'The last transcript will tell you.'

'It was only three days before he took his own life. He didn't say anything to you?'

'No.'

'Not even about my visit?'

Naylor rolled his eyes up. 'Can't remember.'

Which probably meant 'no.' 'You give me straight answers or we can continue this conversation at the station.'

Naylor's expression dropped.

'And what about the diary?'

Naylor didn't react.

'You know about that?'

He shook his head at Fabian.

Banner pocketed her phone. 'Surely he would have mentioned that to you. Seeing as you were his confidant.'

'He might have.' Naylor blinked as if trying to remember. He stopped fidgeting.

Fabian couldn't work out if it was a desperate attempt to establish he had an intimate rapport with Wisher or plain prevarication. 'Did he or not?'

'He was always writing. You'll have to give me a few more details.'

'None of which you'll be able to use on your blog, *Ainsley*.' Banner warned. 'Understand?'

'Of course.' Naylor struggled upright in his chair.

'Diary entries for May to August. Ring any bells?' Fabian fixed him.

There wasn't any indication that he knew Fabian had given him the wrong dates.

'No.'

'And you've never met a woman named Nadine James?' Fabian didn't blink and nor did Naylor.

'Never.'

'What were you doing this afternoon at about two o'clock?' He held his gaze.

'I was here,' Naylor replied, as if he wouldn't be anywhere else. 'What is this?'

'At this desk?' Banner folded her arms.

'Yes. Playing Parapet with about six other players. I can give you their details.'

'Yes, we'll definitely need those,' she said sharply.

Naylor blenched and discreetly swallowed.

Fabian speculated as to when the last time an adult had raised a voice to him might have been. Wait, he *was* an adult. 'And your mother will confirm this?'

'Yeah – um – she might have been in work.'

'Might have been?' Fabian sighed.

'Or shopping. I think she goes shopping on Mondays.'

Fabian doubted that Naylor had any concept of what it took for his mother to maintain the roof over his head let alone keep him in Cheetos. 'Has Wisher ever given you anything?'

Naylor pursed his lips. 'Only interviews.'

'I'd like you to compile a file for me. Transcripts, your own writing about Wisher, anything that's relevant, email it to me.' Banner handed Naylor her card.

'It's copyrighted material.'

'Anything that's relevant,' she repeated. 'By tomorrow morning.'

'I've got other things on my plate.'

'Another Parapet marathon?' Fabian opened his palms. 'We could seize your computer. Your choice.'

Fabian and Banner were silent as Naylor glowered at them.

'All right,' he huffed.

Banner lowered her tone. 'So, really, why the obsession with Wisher?'

Naylor scrutinised the carpet.

'Ainsley?' she prompted.

Fabian could see that bringing up a teenage boy had stood Banner in good stead.

'He had no reason to do any of it.'

The immediacy and conviction of his answer chilled Fabian. 'What d'you mean by that?' But he already knew.

'He didn't have a bad upbringing. He wasn't abused. He had everything he wanted. But he went ahead and killed those people. For a while, he did exactly what his instincts told him to. Was happy to see out his sentence for that brief freedom.'

'And you admired him for that?' Banner said, flatly.

'Out here all we're told about is consequences.'

Fabian assumed 'out here' meant anything that wasn't within the virtual walls where it appeared Naylor spent the majority of his time.

'Chris didn't care about them.'

'But he's not happy to see out his sentence. He's killed himself.' Banner reminded him.

'He must have been *very* ill. Probably something hardcore. Makes sense if he didn't want to be around to suffer.'

'So, he was a role model as well as a friend?' Banner couldn't hide her incredulity.

'Read the transcripts. Without prejudice. Chris was leading his life in a way most of us are afraid to.'

'Murdering people?' Fabian wondered if he'd underestimated Naylor.

'We all think about doing that.'

'Do we?' Banner shook her head.

'I'm talking about us.' Naylor nodded at Fabian.

'Men?' Banner snorted.

'Don't include me in that.' Fabian folded his arms now.

Naylor showed Fabian his teeth. 'You probably would have strangled *Chris* if you'd had half the chance.'

CHAPTER SEVENTEEN

Jennifer Keene lived in a flat above a Lebanese restaurant in Balham High Road. She led Fabian and Banner up a tight, dingy staircase to a battered yellow door at the top. There was a delicious smell of cooking in the atmosphere but when they entered her tiny living space it was clear the spicy aroma was coming from downstairs.

The orange curtains were drawn and the stark lights highlighted the grubby pea green walls and beige carpet. Furnishings were sparse and there was a small open kitchen area by a frosted glass back door that led out onto a fire escape.

Jennifer had been hidden by the shadows when she'd opened the door to them so as she turned they both took her in properly. She was tall, her shoulder-length hair was shaggy and dyed a deep purple and it accentuated her pale features as much as her dark eye make-up. Her slender face was attractive but already set into a scowl. She was dressed in a red Royal Mail sweatshirt, dark trousers and leather shoes.

'How long is this going to take? I need to take a shower. Long day at the sorting office.'

Fabian guessed the bathroom was tucked off behind the door beside the grease-spattered oven. 'As the officer who phoned you explained, I'd just like to ask you a few questions about your visits to Christopher Wisher.'

'Why? He's dead now,' she said matter-of-factly and sniffed.

'Were you upset by that news?' Banner undid her claret parka.

Jennifer's brown eyes darted to her. 'Don't think it's properly sunk in yet.' She moved a basket of dirty washing from the couch. 'You going to sit down?'

'Thank you.' Fabian sat first.

Banner followed. 'And were you surprised by it?'

Jennifer sat in a small studded leather chair with no arms and circled her hands around her legs defensively. 'I'd been waiting for it. Ever since he told me about his condition.'

Fabian figured she had his confidence more than Naylor. 'When did he tell you he was ill?'

'Couple of months ago.' She eyed the patch of empty seat between them.

'And did he say anything to you about what was to happen after his death?' Fabian watched her gaze remain fixed.

'No. I only visited him once more after that.'

Fabian knew that to be true. 'Why was that? You'd been his most frequent visitor.'

'It was too painful. I don't think he wanted me to see him deteriorate.'

'Did you notice that begin to happen?' Fabian registered a gold necklace with her first name dangling from it over the collar of her red top.

'He got very morose.'

He cleared his throat. 'Would you say you had an intimate relationship with Mr Wisher?'

She looked up and nodded once.

'We've been talking to a man named Bruce or Ainsley Naylor.'

'What the hell for?' She shook her head at him in exasperation.

'We're speaking to everyone who visited Christopher Wisher,' Banner placated.

'You won't get any sense out of that fat leech.'

Fabian sat forward. 'I understand you two have had some heated exchanges.'

'No, I've never spoken to him.'

He frowned. 'But he said you trolled him.'

'He's a liar. But then lying is all he does.'

'Why do you say that?'

'All those transcripts of conversations he said he's had with Chris, he makes all of them up.'

'But we know that Naylor visited him on a number of occasions.' Banner said first.

'That *is* true. But he's just a sad fan boy. He could barely string a sentence together when he was in Chris's presence let alone conduct an interview.'

'So how would you categorise *yourself*?' Fabian challenged.

'What do you mean?'

'If you think Naylor was a leech and a fan boy what title are you comfortable with?'

'Girlfriend,' she said to him, as if there couldn't be any doubt.

'Is that what *he* called you?' Banner enquired innocently.

Jennifer thought about it. 'I don't think he ever had any reason to.'

'But, as far as you were concerned, you had that relationship.' Fabian wondered how she was going to justify it. 'Naylor told us that you claimed to have had sex with Wisher.'

She snorted. 'That would have been impossible but I *was* able to satisfy him.'

'How?' He looked past the heavy mascara on her lashes.

'Under the table. I learned to improvise. I used my foot to touch him,' she declared, casually.

That sounded highly unlikely to Fabian. 'You were never caught?'

'I was always very discreet.'

'So why exactly were you drawn to him?' Banner couldn't quite keep the exasperation out of her question.

'Why the interrogation?'

'We'll get to that. Can you just answer the Detective Sergeant's question.'

'It started with *Urban Predator*. After the first episode I was compelled to watch you and the outcome of the investigation.' Her attention locked on Fabian. 'But the identity of the man you were hunting, that was even more fascinating. And when I saw Chris's arrest I knew that his family would reject him and that he'd be all alone.'

Fabian wondered if that was what had happened to Jennifer before she'd convinced herself of her new purpose.

'I reached out to him when I knew nobody else would.'

Banner interrupted, 'Even though he was a cold-blooded murderer.'

'And a human being.' Jennifer emphasised.

Fabian eyed the necklace. 'Why were you not terrified of him?'

'That was everybody else's job.' She noticed what Fabian was looking at and rubbed her gold name between her thumb and forefinger. 'He gave me this,' she said, as if it were an engagement ring.

'*Gave* you it?' he repeated incredulously.

'I told him about it and he said I should buy it.'

Fabian wondered if she was completely deluded about Wisher's feelings for her. 'And did he shower you with any other gifts?'

Either she chose to ignore the comment or was oblivious to its sceptical tone. 'Nobody knew what we had.'

Which was very handy, thought Fabian.

Banner was scrolling through her phone. 'You've blogged a lot about your feelings for him but you rarely mention anything you discussed.'

'That was private. Between him and me.'

Banner chewed her lip. 'And did he talk about any of the other visitors he spoke to?'

'No.'

Her finger paused on her iPhone screen. 'But how would you know that Naylor was tongue-tied in his presence?'

Jennifer narrowed her eyes at her. 'He chatted generally but I meant that he never told me about what they discussed.'

'Weren't you curious? Maybe a little jealous?'

She returned her attention to Fabian. 'Jealous?'

'Of Naylor's access? And there was another woman who visited him.'

'No there wasn't,' she was categorical.

'Yes.' Banner opened her notes. 'Naomi Peel.'

Her dark eyes darted. 'He never mentioned her.'

'Visited him thirteen times,' Banner confirmed.

'She must be… a relation.' Jennifer seemed to be raking her memory banks for the name.

'Nope.' Banner pocketed her phone.

'Who is she then?' Jennifer demanded.

Fabian raised his eyebrows at her sudden flare-up. 'We'll be interviewing her in due course.'

'Are you going to tell me what this is about now?'

Twenty minutes later, Jennifer showed them out and followed them down the stairs into the dark hallway. 'Will you need to speak to me again?'

'It's very likely.' Fabian turned the knob of the front door and let some orange streetlight in.

'We'll be in touch with you once we've spoken to the lido.' Banner walked into the street.

Fabian thanked her for her time and she closed the door on him. Jennifer Keene had an alibi for her lunch hour that day, if it checked out. She was an avid outdoor swimmer and had been doing lengths of Tooting Lido with three friends. Like Naylor she claimed never to have heard of Nadine James.

'Thoughts?' He followed Banner back to the car on the other side of the street.

'Fantasist?' Banner halted for a delivery bike to pass by.

'But she did actually spend time with Wisher.'

'I don't think she did in the way she told us. Foot jobs under the table?'

'Why lie about it?'

'Maybe now Wisher's dead she's seen an opportunity to exploit it. She could make a lot of money selling her story. Certainly more than she gets from sorting the mail.'

'And Naylor is her competition. He's the only other person who's blogging about his access. Although it sounds like he's been embroidering his conversations.' Fabian unlocked the car with the remote key.

'She seemed surprised to hear about Naomi Peel. Almost as if Wisher had been unfaithful to her.'

Fabian looked briefly back to the glowing curtained window over the restaurant. 'Maybe neither she nor Naylor got what they needed from Wisher and concocted their own version of the relationship they wanted to have.'

'Very possible. And Naylor said they'd exchanged hostilities.'

'Yes, I think Jennifer lied about that although if Naylor was trolled it's possible he assumed it was her when it might not have been.'

'Maybe.' Banner stopped at the car. 'I think we have to question the motives of anyone who chooses to visit a serial killer, though.'

'So we have Naomi Peel left and…'

'A man called Ronan Fuller. Criminologist.'

Fabian opened the driver's door. 'Saving it all for the book, probably.'

Banner circled around to her side. 'He lives off Clapham Common but he's lecturing in Edinburgh tonight. Naomi is out of the country until tomorrow.'

'Let's go and talk to them first thing then.' Fabian got in, closed the door, slid on his belt and started the engine.

Banner slammed her door after her. 'It could have been you.'

'Meaning?'

'That Jennifer fixated on. Almost was, by the sound of it. You've got Christopher Wisher to thank for the fact she wasn't stalking you.'

'At least I'd get any suspect packages delivered first class.'

Banner smiled dourly and tugged on her belt.

Fabian pulled out into the traffic, headed along the high road and wondered if they were wasting valuable time interviewing people who were the most obvious suspects. But who else might have a connection to Wisher who would carry out his instructions with such brutal conviction, somebody from way back in his past? And how would he have communicated the dates in the diary to anyone other than visitors to Kerslake Prison?

CHAPTER EIGHTEEN

Ronan Fuller's double-fronted Edwardian home was in an exclusive cul-de-sac in Nightingale Triangle on the south side of Clapham Common. Fabian noted the open garage with a yellow, a dark blue and a red car parked up, all with 2018 number plates. A straw-haired little girl of about three wearing a plastic cooking apron and a broad Ribena smile opened the pristine red door.

'Emmeline, you have to wait for Mummy before you answer the front door.'

The harassed platinum blonde woman who quickly brought up the rear was in denim dungarees. Fabian put her around late thirties. 'Mrs Fuller?'

'Go back to Nadia,' she ordered her daughter. 'Quick, she's about to take the croissants out of the oven.' She watched her race back down the hall runner. 'Sorry, chaotic morning. Come in.'

Fabian entered with Banner behind. They were in a spotless white hallway that had an antique rocking chair at the bottom of the stairs. He could smell the pastries and see down to the large kitchen at the end. Emmeline joined her older sister on a stool at the island counter where a slim woman he assumed to be their nanny was taking a tray from the eye-level oven.

'He's expecting you but he's just taking a call. Knock on the door.' She indicated the closed one to their right.

Fabian regarded it. 'Thank you.'

But Mrs Fuller was already trotting back to the kitchen.

Fabian raised his knuckles to the panel but it opened and Ronan Fuller was standing there. He had a threadbare grey cardigan on but despite his slightly dishevelled appearance his salt and pepper hair and goatee beard were trimmed neatly. His skin was deeply tanned and his thin gold specs perfectly framed his piercing green gaze.

'Sorry about that, just finished a call. Come in.' Fuller turned and walked back into his spacious and traditional office.

Fabian and Banner followed him. The back wall was entirely covered by bookshelves and through the open plantation blinds of the window to their left was an expansive garden.

'I'm Detective Inspector Fabian and this is Detective Sergeant Banner, thanks for giving up your time.'

'No problem.' Fuller seated himself behind his long mahogany desk and hit a key on his laptop before closing the lid. He gestured to the two seats that were positioned in front of him.

Fabian sat and so did Banner. 'You've conducted several interviews with Christopher Wisher?'

'Yes. The last one was around mid-September.'

Fabian watched him interlink his hands on top of the closed laptop and noticed he wore a large onyx ring on the little finger of his left hand. 'Can I ask what the purpose of those interviews was?'

'I'm just completing the first draft of a book about him.'

'A biography?'

'No, a study of the eight months from his first homicide to his arrest, although biographical details form part of my analysis.'

'And he was happy to participate?'

'Very willing. Although he could be a little… capricious.'

'In what way?'

'Sometimes he was very responsive to my questions, other times not. Are you familiar with my work?' Fuller's eyes flitted to the row of tomes book ended by two brass cherub figurines to the back right of his desk.

'I'm afraid not.'

'My principal interest is in motivation, not a subject's capture, catalysts for criminal behaviour and not the nature of their apprehension, although he did often ask after your well-being.'

Fabian felt a bubble rise. 'And what did you tell him?'

'That I knew very little.'

'Very little?'

'That you were still working homicide. That was all the info I could give him.'

Fabian counted how long it took Fuller to blink. He got to nine before he did. 'And what were your conclusions about Wisher?'

Fuller briefly tightened his lips. 'I'm still meditating on those.'

'I thought you said you'd nearly finished a first draft,' Banner said. 'Surely you must have arrived at some by now?'

He regarded her for the first time. 'I have several but I think they may be the ones Wisher wanted me to arrive at.'

'Would you mind allowing the Detective Sergeant and I to see the book?'

Panic skimmed through Fuller's gaze but he quickly composed himself. 'I'm still editing. Shifting material around.'

'That doesn't matter.' Fabian waved a dismissive hand. 'And I take it you recorded your conversations with Wisher?'

Fuller nodded once, as if reluctant to admit it.

'Would you mind releasing them to us?'

'Uh, no.' Fuller waggled uncomfortably in his swivel chair. 'Everything's in disarray but I'll attempt to collate the audio files I have. Could take some time, though.'

'Excellent.' Fabian could tell Fuller was delaying. 'I appreciate you letting us take a look, even if it's unpolished.'

'So this is more than just an investigation into his suicide?' Fuller flitted his green eyes between both of them.

Fabian nodded. 'And how did you feel when you heard about his death?'

Fuller seemed at a loss for words. 'Well…'

Fabian wondered if Fuller realised he should have shown more emotion. 'Surprised?'

Fuller considered the word. 'Yes. Not that he hadn't spoke of suicide before…'

'He had?' Fabian exchanged a look with Banner.

'It cropped up in our discussions. Suicide is a constant spectre in prison, particularly for criminals serving life sentences. But I was surprised Wisher took his own life.'

'Why?'

'He was always so composed. Didn't appear to struggle with prison. He seemed very philosophical about the time he was serving.'

'So you didn't know about his illness?'

'No…'

'Brain cancer.' Fabian watched Fuller slightly shake his head. The revelation had barely disturbed his features though. 'He knew he had little time before the condition overtook him.'

'I guess what he said at our last meeting makes sense then.'

'Which was?' Fabian's attention was drawn to the window. Fuller's children were running towards the swings at the end of the garden with Nadia trailing behind them.

'He told me that our September session would be his last.'

'That didn't ring any alarm bells?'

'Not really. I'd obtained most of what I'd needed and Wisher had become increasingly withdrawn from questioning. I presumed he'd grown tired of me.'

'So he no longer cared you were writing a book about him?'

'His attitude changed. His illness might explain that. What was his prognosis?'

'We're going to find that out when we speak to his doctor. Did Wisher ever mention anyone else outside of the prison that he was in touch with?'

'No. So, when are you going to tell me what this is about?'

'A woman was murdered in Battersea Park yesterday and it was Wisher's MO – broad daylight, mutilation of the body and a dead bird was found next to the body.' Fabian assessed Fuller's reaction. There was no immediate shock.

'A copycat killing?' Fuller seemed more intrigued than horrified.

Fabian wondered if Fuller was considering the news as a promotional opportunity. 'That remains between us for the moment, Mr Fuller, and we'd appreciate your discretion.'

Fuller nodded emphatically. 'Of course.'

'So, Wisher didn't mention anyone else he was in contact with?'

'No.' He answered a little too quickly.

A child's shout shifted Fabian and Banner's attention briefly to the window.

Fabian noted that Fuller seemed too lost in their conversation to register the noise. 'What about a man named Sean Coles?' The suspect in the rape and murder of rent boy Rodney Trent was a long shot.

Fuller pursed his lips. 'No. Who was he?'

'We're not sure if he's relevant just yet.'

The little girl's screams got more frequent but Fuller still didn't acknowledge them.

'Sounds lively.' Banner watched the two girls fighting.

'Nadia is with them,' Fuller said dismissively, as if it was a common scenario.

Fabian noticed that their mother wasn't out there. 'Were you at home with your family yesterday afternoon?'

Fuller nodded and then realised what he was being asked. 'Am I a suspect?'

'We're interviewing everyone who has been in contact with Wisher. I assume you can account for your whereabouts.'

'Yes.' Fuller seemed to think that would be sufficient but Fabian's silence said otherwise. 'We took the girls to a party in Croydon. Nadia was with us.'

'D'you mind if we have a word with them on our way out?'

'Of course not.' Fuller clenched his hands tighter on his laptop.

Fabian thought his reaction was normal. Innocent people often got nervous even if they did have an ironclad alibi. It was those who were a hundred per cent confident he was more suspicious of. 'Would you say Wisher trusted you?'

'Enough to allow me glimpses of his thought processes.'

'During the time he killed?'

Fuller nodded. 'He said he always felt removed from the procedure. That he looked upon it as a feat of engineering.'

'Engineering?' Banner repeated for them both.

'And making incisions in their stomachs and putting his hand inside them, that was part of his "procedure"?' Fabian failed to keep the scorn from his voice.

'He maintained it was entirely mechanical. He said the gratification came much later, when he saw the outcome of what he described as a period of inconvenience.'

Neither of them responded.

'He said he entirely bypassed himself when he took people's lives.'

'And his selections were arbitrary?' Fabian suddenly felt as if the dynamic had changed and wondered if Fuller took satisfaction from the fact that he'd learned more than they had during endless hours of interrogation.

'He researched locations rather than people. Places where he could work undisturbed. Then he'd wait to see who passed through.'

'But why always in the daylight?' Banner was as eager for answers.

'He said he felt it authenticated him. He looked upon darkness as a cheap tool. The refuge of the amateur. But killing in plain sight was something he thought he'd only experience once or twice before he was caught. He said he always wanted to be captured. Felt he was endangering his family and that harming them was his greatest fear.'

'But his activities took away the thing that was the most precious to him,' Banner argued.

Fabian agreed. 'And if he wanted to save his family why did he not hand himself in after he murdered his first victim?'

'I'm only quoting what he told me. I personally believe that he enjoyed murdering his victims. Wisher was always in control of what he did. I think he had the same emotional bypass when it came to his family. He never spoke of how much he missed them.'

'Perhaps segregating himself was what he thought was best for them.' Banner's attention went back to the children outside.

Fuller shook his head. 'Everything he did domestically was like the engineering he spoke of. I think murdering was when he really allowed himself to exist.'

'Was it me or did it sound like Fuller admired Wisher more than Naylor or Keene?' Banner lowered her voice as they walked back down the driveway to where Fabian's Audi was parked.

'Looks like he's built a career inserting himself into the heads of psychopaths.'

'But how easy is it to pull yourself out of there, leave it all in the office while you have dinner with your family?'

Fabian recalled how oblivious Fuller had been to his own children. 'That's something we can both relate to. Or are your instincts telling you something else?'

'I don't know. Perhaps it's bothering me he managed to get answers we never could.'

'And what did Wisher get from it?'

'Another ego massage?'

'Wisher was skilled at manipulation. It was how he got his victims alone. Maybe he persuaded Fuller to do more than be his transcriber.'

She pulled her collar around her neck. 'But it looks like his alibi checks out. His wife, children, the nanny; all said he was with them.'

Fabian believed them as well. But Fuller's lack of emotion across their entire dialogue had made him uneasy. 'And he seemed reluctant to release his work.'

'Perhaps he's precious about us seeing a raw draft.'

'Let's make sure he doesn't drag his heels with that manuscript or the audio files.'

'I'll chase them after we've interviewed Naomi Peel.'

'Sounds like he might have to add a few new chapters before he's done anyway,' Fabian said, bleakly.

CHAPTER NINETEEN

'Ms Peel?'

The fifty-something woman sitting in the office Fabian and Banner walked into looked up from her screen, smiled and shook her head at him. 'No, I'll just let her know you're here.' She was about to get up when a door behind her opened.

'Thanks, Steff.' Naomi Peel was in her late forties and wearing a sharp dark blue suit. Her hair was silver grey and cut into a stylish bob and she had large blue-rimmed specs that sat in the middle of her heavily made-up square face. 'Come in.' She held her door for them to enter.

Fabian nodded thanks to the receptionist and stepped into the office. Naomi Peel's dewberry scent hung subtly in the room.

'Coffee?'

'No, thanks.' Despite the height of her heels she was barely chest height. Compact and attractive, she immediately exuded confidence and, given the plush office and the Wardour Street address, Fabian assumed the temp agency she'd run for eleven years was thriving.

Peel raised her eyebrows at Banner.

'No, thanks.'

She gestured them to a couch against the wall and after they'd sat down settled herself in a swivel chair in front of her desk. 'It was quite a shock to hear about Christopher. And I know it was for Patricia.'

'You knew Wisher's wife?' Banner confirmed.

Peel nodded.

Fabian could see the distress in her eyes. 'Can I ask why you visited Mr Wisher at Kerslake Prison?'

'I'm a friend of the family. Have been since… 2001.'

'And how did that come about?'

'When I moved to Richmond I was six doors down from them. They used to have community parties in the close – royal occasions, summer fêtes. I got to know the Wishers that way. My daughter went out with their son for a few months.'

'Liam?' Banner took out her phone.

'Yes. It didn't last long. It was sweet for a while but he was three years older than her. You know what boys are like.'

Fabian watched her interlink her fingers and rest them in her lap. 'You still live there?'

'No. We moved to Hampstead Heath five years ago but I stayed in touch with Patricia.'

'*And* Mr Wisher?'

She nodded, looked guarded. 'Yes. We still visited the family.'

'You and your partner?' Fabian asked.

'No, it's just Lily and me. Has been since she was seven.'

He wondered how difficult it had been to juggle motherhood with her career. 'So why the regular visits to Kerslake?'

'As a favour to Patricia,' she answered immediately.

'But haven't the family suspended all connection with him?' Banner crossed her leg.

She nodded. 'Yes but she still needed to communicate with him about financial affairs. He always handled that side of things so a lot of policies were in his name.'

Sounded like a big ask to Fabian. 'Couldn't solicitors have done that for her?'

'She couldn't afford them. Patricia had stopped working. Had something of a breakdown and spent months trying to sell the house.'

'So you offered to speak with Wisher on her behalf?'

She nodded once at Fabian. 'I wanted to help her.'

But Fabian noticed she'd briefly clamped her lips before answering. 'Despite what he'd done?'

'She was in a terrible state. And I was concerned about Liam. He was about to start college when Christopher was arrested. He began drinking… and doing other things. Patricia had her hands full just trying to keep him from harming himself.'

Fabian wondered if she was deflecting. 'Are you talking about suicide?'

'There were episodes. He just went off the rails. Patricia said despite therapy he got a lot of attention after the trial. A lot of the kids at college wanted to get to know the son of a serial killer. I think he used it to his advantage but despised himself for it at the same time.'

'So you agree to visit a man who you thought you knew well, somebody who murdered and mutilated nine people.'

Peel regarded him warily, had caught the scepticism in the question.

'You must have been terrified.' Banner prompted, her tone sympathetic.

'He was still the person I'd known. Nothing had changed when we spoke.'

'But didn't you consider you could have been one of his victims? If he'd had the opportunity?'

She hardly reacted, simply regarded Fabian as if his comment was so misinformed it wasn't worth responding to.

Banner pushed on. 'Did he ask after his family?'

'No. He was always happy to sign whichever papers I took to him but he never enquired after Patricia or Liam.'

'Did you ever try to tell him about the pain he was putting them through?' Fabian watched her hands separate and rest lightly on the chrome arms of the chair.

'He never gave me an opening for that. It was like a business meeting. A very informal one but as if the reason for us being there didn't exist.'

'And why do you think that was?' Fabian was sure she concealing something more personal.

'I think he'd blocked it. He knew there were practicalities that had to be addressed but maybe it was easier for him to banish his family from his mind.'

'How was he with them?' Fabian noticed her cheeks had started to flush under her make-up. 'When you used to live in the neighbourhood?'

'He wasn't tactile with Patricia. Certainly not with his son but Liam was at that awkward age. Hated either of them coming near him. Christopher was a little stiff but always making jokes. Poking good-natured fun.'

'He made you laugh?'

She showed him her palms. 'Yes.'

Banner waited for her to finger away her fringe. 'And what did your daughter have to say about Liam?'

'She had a crush on him. I think he looked out for her more than anything else. Like a brother. But I'm sure that was because he was scared of me.'

'Scared?' Banner repeated.

'I disciplined my daughter. Liam was very spoilt. He never misbehaved when he came into my house, though. He started dating somebody his own age from school then so we didn't see him any more.'

'And you socialised with Wisher, during the time he was murdering people?'

She only nodded at Fabian, her face blank.

Fabian was a little puzzled. 'And he immediately agreed to see you at Kerslake? Even though you'd moved away from the area?'

'As I said, I always stayed in touch with Patricia.'

'And likewise her husband?'

'I still saw him. Yes.' She started to show her irritation with Fabian's questions.

'So, how long did it take to sort out Patricia's business affairs?'

She seemed overly baffled by Fabian's question.

'It's just you visited Wisher thirteen times, over a period of thirty months. All the way up to last month. What specifically were you executing on Patricia's behalf?'

'Literally nothing was in her name. Every document had to be amended and countersigned.'

'But it sounds like he was more than willing to do this. And your visits were never short of the full hour. That's a lot of signatures.'

'We had other conversations.'

'About?' Fabian watched her attempt to discreetly swallow.

'He always had questions.'

'Not about his family. We've established that. What did you fill all that time talking about?'

Peel bit her lip then seemed to come to a decision about something. 'Look, I was visiting him before Patricia asked me to.'

That was a significant omission. But Fabian had guessed why. 'Had you been intimate with Wisher in the past?'

'Briefly,' she responded reluctantly.

'And was Patricia aware of that?' Banner's tone remained level.

'I don't think so.'

'When was this?' Fabian was in no mood for further evasion. 'Before you moved from the neighbourhood?'

'No. Afterwards. Chris, Christopher…' she checked herself '… helped me to move. That's when it happened.'

'Once?' He wondered how often she considered where being alone with Wisher could have led.

'Several times. It ended about a month after.'

'You ended it or he did?'

Her gaze hardened. 'It was a mutual decision.'

'Because of your children?' Banner interjected.

'Yes.' But Peel seemed glad of the prompt.

'And even after his arrest and the subsequent revelations you still wanted to see him?' Fabian raised an eyebrow.

'I knew Patricia refused to.'

'Morbid fascination? Or did you still have feelings for him?'

She shook her head, as if Fabian's question was something she'd been trying to answer herself. 'He was alone. Abandoned. I still couldn't believe he'd done the things they said he had.'

Banner sat forward. 'So you needed to hear it from him?'

'He'd confessed. There was no doubt. But I still couldn't process it. That a man who had been so tender with me…'

But Fabian wasn't convinced. 'Did you know about his diagnosis?'

She eventually nodded.

'And what were your feelings about that? And his suicide?' He couldn't detect a trace of them in her expression.

'It was a relief.'

'For whom? The families of the people he murdered or were you glad that *he* didn't have to suffer?'

'He was ill. A sane man couldn't have done the things he did.'

Fabian couldn't believe that somebody could be so self-deluded. 'He was diagnosed after starting his sentence.'

'But who knows how long he had the tumour?' But she still kept her emotions in check.

'Brain cancer didn't make him kill, Ms Peel.'

'You know that for sure? Locking away a problem doesn't solve it. Maybe you should be more interested in making a documentary about *that*.'

Fabian considered how Naomi Peel hadn't even been on his radar during the inquiry. Yet here was a significant person in Wisher's life who had been unable to do anything except watch things unfold from a distance. Until the spotlight had shifted away and she'd contacted him at Kerslake. 'Did Wisher talk to you about the other woman who came to see him?'

She eyed him suspiciously and didn't reply.

'Jennifer Keene?' Because of her online presence Fabian would be surprised if she weren't aware of her.

'I understood she had an infatuation with him.'

'Something that he indulged.' He watched her whole body tense.

'He welcomed anyone who wanted to visit him. There weren't many candidates.'

'Sounds like there were enough. Did you approve?' Fabian detected the opposite.

'Of what?'

'Jennifer. She told us she was physical with Wisher.'

'Lies. That would have been impossible.'

Fabian could tell there was more anger in her dismissal than she wanted to reveal. 'So you never touched him when you visited?'

'No.'

'Did you want to?'

'Of course not.'

'But you had that history with him.'

'That's exactly what it was… history.'

'So if he was getting a foot job from Jennifer Keene you wouldn't be bothered one way or the other.' Fabian knew using the detail would provoke a reaction.

'No,' she responded, tight-lipped.

'You were visiting him because you wanted to satisfy your curiosity about somebody who had freely admitted to murdering and mutilating his victims.'

'As I explained, I was there on behalf of his family.' She glowered at Fabian.

He let her do that for a few moments longer. 'So were you disappointed that you weren't his only visitor?'

'No. People fixate. But it was social interaction. He needed that.'

'He didn't forge any friendships with other inmates then?' Banner put her phone on the arm of the couch.

'No. He stayed in his cell as much as possible. Even had his meals there.'

'Is that because one of his victims was a teenager? Often makes a prisoner a target.' Fabian still couldn't accept that an intelligent woman like her would still put herself in Wisher's presence.

'She was nineteen.'

'Barely.' He jogged her memory. How could she even try to mitigate by quibbling over Natalie Spence's age. 'And how old is your daughter, Lily?'

'She's seventeen now.' She knew where he was going.

'How would you be, identifying her body two years from now?'

'Why are you grilling me like this? It was my choice to visit him. It's not a crime.'

'But replicating his murders is. And we believe that's exactly what somebody is doing.'

Her face responded accordingly, mouth hanging slightly open.

But Fabian wasn't sure if her expression was a little too stunned. 'So you'll understand why we have more questions for you about your activities yesterday.'

'This is absurd…' She blinked, as if she were snapping out of a trance.

'What is?' He could see her knuckles whiten as she gripped the arms of the chair. 'That a woman has been murdered or that a person unfazed by a man who kills for pleasure and repeatedly visited him under the guise of helping his wife could possibly be a suspect?'

As Fabian and Banner went down in the lift he pointed at her phone. 'We check with The Veridian as soon as possible.'

Banner nodded.

Naomi Peel had told them she'd been attending a conference at the hotel in Frankfurt the previous afternoon.

'She must be in complete denial,' Banner commented.

Fabian shook his head. 'How could you retain any sort of feelings for somebody who did what Wisher did?'

'You think she might have known what Wisher was doing while they were an item?'

It had immediately occurred to Fabian. 'She didn't really tell us why they broke it off.'

'It's certainly not the behaviour of someone who was duped by Wisher.'

'Perhaps he's just become an obsession for her. Like he has for others. Particularly as she had a past connection with him.'

The lift shuddered to a halt and Banner stepped to the door. 'That would be something I'd do my utmost to forget.'

'Maybe we should talk to Patricia Wisher again. Find out if anyone has tried to contact her since she relocated. She had plenty of stalkers beforehand.'

'Poor woman.' Banner shook her head. 'Even after Wisher's death it looks like she and her son will be dragged back into his world again.'

The lift doors opened into the downstairs reception and Banner's phone buzzed. She halted, checked the message that had arrived and bit her lip.

Fabian paused. 'The office?'

'No.' She didn't elaborate.

'Everything OK?'

She nodded.

But Fabian could see distress in her dark eyes. 'If you need some time—'

'I'd rather focus on this at the moment,' she said finally.

Fabian knew better than to push it. But he couldn't help feel that there was something momentous going on. 'I bore you enough about Harriet and Tilly. Feel free to let rip if you need to.'

'I'll remember that, thanks.'

But he could tell that that was the end of the conversation.

CHAPTER TWENTY

It was their fifth date but as Mark Mason walked into McCool's bar Tilly Fabian was still nervous. He was late by exactly fifteen minutes again and she wondered if he deliberately waited that long before making an appearance. *You should be late next time.* She'd said that to herself umpteen times before. Her friends told her she was pathologically punctual.

Mark smiled at her as he crossed the bar and got himself a drink. The jukebox was playing Tom Waits. As he was served he gestured at hers but she shook her head. She already had a Scarlett O'Hara, a cocktail her father had introduced her to – Southern Comfort, lime and cranberry – and she knew she had to take her time. Mark was handed a bottle of beer and paid the barman.

She'd have to closely monitor his intake as well. He freely admitted that a few Kronenbourgs was his limit. Mark Mason was many things but an experienced drinker wasn't one of them. That endeared him to her even more though and she'd enjoyed putting him to bed after their fourth date. That was the most intense things had got so far but Tilly felt slightly guilty that she might have taken advantage of him. She hadn't slept with him, however, had remained at least partially clothed.

When she'd assured her parents that her studies would come first she'd believed it herself. But a month into her first term at Exeter Uni and biosciences were already becoming an inconvenience. Tilly balked at what a cliché student she'd so quickly become. Her parents had allowed her a gap year because she'd convinced them she needed the break before she knuckled down for the foreseeable. Having only just finished with her boyfriend of two years she hadn't expected herself to even be aware of the male students but now here she was nursing feelings that slightly scared her.

In her defence, Mark had approached her at the open day. Told her there were better places than campus to drink and that he knew Exeter if she needed a guide. She'd still been with her other boyfriend then and had resisted thinking about him. But Tilly knew that Mark, as well as her moving away, had been instrumental in finishing her previous relationship.

Mark wasn't tall; only taller than her by an inch or two. He wasn't muscular either. He didn't dress particularly well. She'd have a word with him about the teal cheesecloth shirt he was wearing. Some guys could carry them off, he couldn't. She also felt his dark, shoulder length auburn hair needed shortening but then Tilly was still in two minds about her own henna dyed bob.

But Mark carried something in his expression, an amused intelligence that was alluring and slightly familiar. She'd read somewhere that feeling you knew someone as well as being attracted to them and wanting to protect them all at the same time was the beginnings of... Tilly inhaled as he approached her tall table. She'd chosen it because it was the most private. Two high stools across a small surface and tucked snugly in the back corner.

He put his Kronenbourg on the table and took off his green Kirkconnel jacket. Initially Tilly had thought he'd whitened his teeth but had found out they were natural. He knew her mother would be impressed. She'd told Tilly to always look at a man's teeth and shoes. OK, Mark's scruffy boots probably wouldn't pass muster but his potential was indisputable.

'We've got to work fast.' Mark looked at his chunky watch. 'Two-for-ones ends when the band comes on.'

She smiled. 'You should pace yourself.'

He grinned and looked chastened. 'I told you. It was because I drank on an empty stomach.' But his features said he knew the excuse was lame.

He lifted himself onto his stool and suddenly he was at very close quarters to Tilly. She felt a rush of warmth up the back of her neck and hoped it hadn't registered in her cheeks.

If it did he didn't acknowledge it. 'Fancy eating here?'

Food? She wasn't sure she could. And how could he? Wasn't he experiencing the same dry sickness as her? 'There's no rush.' His familiar scent wafted over Tilly as he settled but there was something else there. Cologne?

'Or do you really want the same outcome?' There was playfulness on his face.

They both knew what it had led to last time.

Tilly felt her cheeks burn. *Please don't let it be too visible.* But it didn't seem to bother Mark. He asked her about her creepy lecturer, Doctor Lockwood; had changed the subject to save her blushes. It was gentlemanly but while they chatted she could see another agenda in his clear blue eyes. How long before they both gave into it?

Mark fought his own nerves. Tilly couldn't see his leg rapidly jigging under the table. She was very easy to be with but slightly intense and her dark brown eyes rarely strayed from his. He occasionally dropped his gaze to her lips as they answered his questions. Had to keep the conversation flowing.

When she asked him about his studies he gave her jokey, succinct responses and turned the chat back to her. He could see she liked that he took an interest in what she was doing at Exeter and didn't suspect at all that he did it because all his answers were lies. He wasn't a chemistry student at Exeter. His name wasn't Mark Mason. It was Liam Wisher.

He knew everything about Tilly Fabian. Had studied her from afar for close to two years before he actually spoke to her at the open day. He'd gleaned from her Facebook page and Twitter feed the sort of guys she liked. The sort of guy he had to be.

Maybe she was looking at him as a fun distraction from her studies. Whatever her intentions, she'd allowed him to get close and that was all he needed. His father had been locked away for three years because of hers. Had just died in his cell. Tom Fabian had become as much a celebrity as Christopher Wisher.

Tilly hadn't discussed her father. They hadn't talked in detail about their parents. It wasn't what you did at this stage. But she would soon know how her life was more connected to his than she suspected.

He wondered when he should start the drunken act. Finish this beer and then give a little sideways stagger when he went to the bathroom? He took a swig from the bottle.

'Where were your lectures today?'

'Reed Hall.' He knew she'd been at Pope House. It was far enough from it so they wouldn't have crossed paths.

'We should hook up for lunch.' She sipped her drink.

'I'd rather be hooking up here.' He smiled and tried to deflect.

Tilly smiled too but looked a little disappointed.

What excuse could he use? 'Have a ton to catch up on this week but maybe next Monday?'

She nodded but tried to be nonchalant. 'I'll see how I'm fixed.'

But if everything went to plan by Monday Tilly wouldn't be so keen. 'How about tonight then? Where shall we go next? Shall we head further into town?'

Tilly glanced at her watch now. 'We could just hang here for a while.'

He caught the mischief in her expression. 'What was the time check for?'

'Ella is going to a club tonight. Says she's leaving at ten.'

'Interesting.' He knew what that meant – Ella gone, room to themselves.

'But we haven't been to your place yet.' She stirred the remainder of her drink with her straw.

She seemed keen to see it. But the student digs he said he shared with three other guys didn't exist. 'If you like crusty socks drying on radiators, you can certainly be my guest.'

'And how many of those are yours?'

'I at least go to the laundrette. Running cold water kills vampires but my flatmates don't realise that their underwear is a different matter.'

Tilly giggled.

'To be avoided at all costs.'

'OK. We'll wait here then and head back into campus. We can pick up a pizza and bottle of wine on the way.' She swigged from her glass and broke eye contact.

He could tell she was trying to be casual about the suggestion and wondered if what she was proposing was a big deal to her. They hadn't had that ex discussion yet but he knew she'd just finished with a long-term boyfriend. How far had it gone with them? 'OK. Sounds good.' He could see Tilly was relieved. It was obviously what she'd hoped for all along. 'Do you want another of those?' He indicated her drink, which was nearly empty.

She nodded and her brown eyes were examining his again. 'When you're ready. No rush.'

But he'd seen how quickly she'd drunk it. It was going to be easy to slip something into her glass. If he did it now her adrenaline would zip it through her system in no time. He would bide his time for the next few days, however. Get closer. Soon she would be completely vulnerable. He was about to go to the bar when her phone rang.

'Hi.' She turned away from him. 'Slightly,' she said, as if she were walking on eggshells.

He assumed the caller had asked if she were busy.

'Yes, I'll be eating.' She turned back and smiled guiltily at him.

It had to be one of her parents.

'Pizza for me, nothing spectacular.' Tilly bit her lip and kept her eyes on him. 'Mum's home tonight. You should call in.'

So it was her father. Tom. He knew her parents were separated. He smirked.

Tilly smirked back. 'Yes, I am in a bar. Just having a drink with Ella.'

He had her lying for him already. He tried to hear Tom Fabian's response but couldn't over the jukebox.

'Yes, I spoke to her today. Why not give her a call yourself?' She huffed a little. 'I've got to go now, Dad. I'll call you on the weekend as usual. I will, bye.' She hung up. 'And the guilt trips begin.'

'Your dad?'

She nodded.

'Cherish them before they're gone.'

Tilly frowned and looked at him quizzically. 'Weren't you getting me a drink?'

He nodded. 'Coming up.'

CHAPTER TWENTY-ONE

Fabian parked his green Audi in the road next to St Jude's Primary School. Pumpkin faces glowed and flickered eerily in the lower windows of the building. It was Halloween and he'd woken that morning awaiting this news.

Banner got out first. On the opposite side of the street police tape demarcated a long row of scaffolding that was clad in misted polythene. Daylight was fading but Fabian could see white figures moving behind it. Further down the pavement two builders in hard hats were giving statements to a female uniformed officer.

They crossed the closed off road and a male uniformed officer lifted the curtain of polythene. They both slipped on foot covers from a box inside and approached the huddle of forensic techs gathered around a body. Two small yellow plastic evidence cones had been positioned just beyond it.

Mills turned and stripped off his blue surgical gloves. 'Another one attacked in broad daylight.'

Fabian looked down at the woman's body, arms positioned above her head. The gaping wound to her throat was almost as deep as her spine, and in the same manner as the last victim and Wisher's nine previous. 'The street must have been busy when she died,' Banner commented.

The victim had on a grey raincoat that was still belted at her waist. There was a deep injury to her abdomen but all the blood had run off the waterproof material and pooled thickly beside the body.

'Who found her?' Fabian asked Mills.

'Site foreman. Work wasn't due to start until next week but he came to do a safety check.

'And we have a definite ID?'

'Polly O'Rourke. She's been missing since this afternoon. Didn't pick up her son from St Jude's but they found her car tucked away at the end of this road. It's being dusted now.' Mills stepped back so Fabian could see the dead blackbird trapped in the thick, congealed blood beside Polly. The first evidence cone was positioned beside it.

'"*Wings clipped.*"' Banner recalled the diary entry.

Fabian turned to the uniformed officer hovering behind them. 'Are you the FOA?'

He nodded.

'What time was Polly meant to have picked up her boy?'

'Three o'clock. There was a parents' meeting but she didn't show.'

'Where's her son now?' Banner asked.

'With his grandparents.'

'Father?' Fabian peered down at the ball peen hammer next to the other cone.

'Not on the scene.'

He turned to Banner. 'What's the next entry?'

She opened the notes on her iPhone. '"Inertia." For two days. Then "*No real tears yet. I'm going to be moved tomorrow though. Have to trust them.*"'

Mills put his hand in the small of his back and grunted. 'Was Wisher ever moved from his cell?'

Fabian shook his head. 'No. He always occupied 29. Maybe we shouldn't waste our time.' Fabian studied the empty street through the scoured polythene.

'With the diary?' Banner said perplexed.

'Remember, Wisher was amusing himself when he wrote it in his cell. He had to make it sound like a prison diary to get it past Briant. They're not specific to the crime scenes and don't give us any latitude to actually prevent the murders. The entries are only intelligible after the event.'

'But they are specific to the date and manner the people are murdered,' she countered.

'Yes, they're a blueprint but we have to focus on finding the person who's putting them into practice and not get waylaid looking for details Wisher couldn't have possibly predicted.'

'You don't think there's a connection between victims?' Mills pocketed his gloves.

'There wasn't with Wisher's previous ones. We have our list of suspects. We have to stay methodical. The only thing we can do is keep working our way through it.'

CHAPTER TWENTY-TWO

'Mr Coles?' But Fabian immediately recognised the man who opened the door to the semi in Raynes Park that evening.

Sean Coles was paunchy, in his sixties, had neatly cut, dyed jet-black hair and was dressed impeccably in a blue blazer, lemon shirt and chino trousers. 'What do you want?' he demanded belligerently.

'I'm Detective Inspector Fabian and this is Detective Sergeant Banner. I'm sorry to disturb you.'

'I'm on my way out to bowls. What's this about?'

Fabian recalled the extent to which Coles had been through the wringer after the rent boy, Rodney Trent, had been found dead in Brompton Cemetery. Fabian hadn't been part of the inquiry but knew that, having been a regular client of Trent's, Coles had become the main suspect. But even though the investigation had found insufficient evidence to convict him, the family life he'd hidden behind had crumbled in its wake. 'Could we step inside?'

Coles gritted his teeth and hissed before standing back to allow them entry.

Fabian noticed him quickly check the houses opposite before closing the door.

'In here,' he snapped and led them to the back lounge.

Fabian and Banner followed him through the salmon pink-carpeted hall and into a large room with a floor-to-ceiling window that looked onto a long, illuminated and immaculately kept lawn.

Fabian didn't believe that Trent's raped and strangulated body bore any hallmarks of a Wisher killing but the dead blackbird that had been found near his corpse had flagged up the murder to a nervous department only three months after Wisher's conviction. The animal looked as if it had been there for some time but once the word 'copycat' had been uttered he'd anticipated a knock on his office door. It had never come and he guessed that the scrutiny the department had received because of his participation in the Wisher documentary had been the reason.

But although the DCI at the time had been at pains to distance the killing from being a Wisher copycat, the perpetrator was never caught and despite the lack of evidence Coles was still very likely to have been responsible. Other rent boys had been interviewed about Coles's taste for sado-masochism and his aggression towards another boy he'd taken to a nearby hotel.

Coles turned and waited, his hands clenched by his sides.

'I'd just like to speak to you about your whereabouts on the 29th of this month and this afternoon.'

'What the hell is this?'

'A murder inquiry and I have to tick boxes. If you can provide me with those details we can quickly eliminate you.'

'A bit desperate, isn't it? Not content with ruining my life once? What did you say your names were?'

Coles had friends in the force. He was a big cheese in his local lodge. Maybe that was another reason why the previous DCI had kept Fabian away from the Brompton case. 'I think you heard the first time, although we're happy to show you our IDs.'

Coles looked through Banner. 'Day before yesterday I was at home all day. This afternoon I was at Man's Chinese restaurant. Buffet lunch. I dropped into The Cavern pub next door afterwards. Speak to the staff in both.'

Banner took out her phone. 'You know them by name?'

'No. You'll have to find that out for yourself. That's your job, isn't it?'

'And what time did you get back?' Fabian asked.

'Sixish.'

'Long lunch,' he commented.

'One of the few perks of being retired.'

Banner quickly typed into her iPhone. 'Were you there with anyone else?'

'Julian Waters.'

'A friend?' Fabian watched his fists tighten.

Coles nodded and sniffed.

Fabian wondered if he was a young friend. 'And where do we contact him?'

He fumbled his mobile out of his pocket, found the number and read it out to Banner.

She repeated it as she keyed it in.

'Is that it then? I've more important things to do with my time.'

Although Coles had a history of unsavoury liaisons Fabian doubted he had anything to do with the death of Nadine James or Polly O'Rourke. 'We'll check these out and be in touch.'

'You know where the door is.' Coles glared at it to remind them.

It was Fabian's first experience of Coles but he couldn't deny he made him suspicious. Something in the way he held himself, how he hovered as if he were nervous of them finding something.

'Thank you for your time,' Banner said as she walked back to the hall.

Fabian nodded to him.

Coles didn't budge. Just kept hovering and scowling as Fabian left the room.

CHAPTER TWENTY-THREE

'Mrs Howman?' Fabian shouted above the motor. It was the morning of Thursday the 1st of November.

The emaciated woman standing on the lawn in her compact front garden switched off the leaf blower.

It wasn't her real surname. She'd changed it after her husband had been convicted. Patricia Wisher had moved to Dorking from their family home in Richmond and started again. The house was a quarter of the size of the one she'd shared with him.

'Thanks for agreeing to see us.' He registered she'd lost at least a couple of stone since the last time he'd seen her. 'You remember Detective Sergeant Banner.'

Patricia was wearing a green wax jacket, jeans and a white bobble hat with an oversized pom-pom. She nodded once and strode over the small lawn towards the open front door.

Fabian and Banner followed.

'Wipe your feet, please.'

They did so and she quickly closed the door behind them. She led them into the kitchen diner at the rear of the property.

Fabian noted how cluttered all the shelves and surfaces were. It looked like she'd tried to fit everything from her large kitchen into her new, smaller one.

'Coffee?' She nodded at the cappuccino machine that was still steaming.

'No, we're good thanks,' Fabian answered.

Patricia seated herself at the wooden kitchen table that looked too big for the room. It was covered by paperwork.

Looked like accounts to Fabian. 'I understand this is a difficult time.'

'My son found out his father was dead on Twitter,' she said to his waist and gestured for them to sit down.

Fabian and Banner pulled out chairs.

'I couldn't reach him at college. Had his phone switched off. Tried him all day but social media beat me.'

'I'm sorry to hear that.' Fabian clasped his hands on the tabletop and waited for her to continue.

She tugged off the bobble hat and dumped it in front of her.

Fabian was shocked. She'd cut her brown curls and her hair was now little more than a shaved tan sheen.

'I still don't know how to react to it.'

Fabian examined her bitten nails. 'Have you seen Liam?'

She shook her head. 'He's busy. I'm glad he is,' she said absently. 'Is he OK?'

'Hard to tell.' She seemed resigned to that. 'I'm the last person he'd open up to.'

In the harsh kitchen strip-light Fabian could see how the ordeal of the past three years had lined her pale, freckled face. She was in her mid-forties but she looked ten years older. 'And how are *you* taking it?'

'Should I feel relief? There's definitely that. But then there's the twenty-two years that I believed he was a good husband and father. And… he was. Should I wipe those from memory as well?'

'Are you still getting counselling?' Banner unzipped her parka.

'Can't afford it. Council tax has to take precedence over my mental well-being.' She squinted at the papers over the desk.

Fabian eyed a pile of bill reminders. 'Maybe this means you can start to get some sort of closure.' He hated how glib that sounded.

'Thanks for saying that.' She briefly grinned, humourlessly. 'I comfort myself by thinking about the families. I hope it's closure for them.' She swallowed. 'I always think of the families.'

Fabian could see she was still in torment. How many times a day did she ask herself why she hadn't seen who Wisher was, could maybe have prevented the deaths of his victims if only she'd been more alert? But Wisher had led the classic double life. Left no clues as to what he did outside the home. No search history, nothing. When he walked in through the front door he was always the man Patricia thought he was. Fabian knew there was no easy way to tell her. 'There's been an unpleasant development since his death.'

Patricia frowned, her expression entirely oblivious to what that could be but immediately fearful of it.

Fabian told her about the deaths of Nadine James and Polly O'Rourke, the birds found near their bodies and the diary her husband had given him that had portended the murders. He watched her features slump and Patricia close her eyes tight.

'Patricia?' Banner said gently.

She opened them again.

Fabian saw a new pain there. 'It has to be somebody he was communicating with from prison.'

'I haven't seen him since that last day in court.'

Banner went to the sink and got her a glass of water.

'We understand you used Naomi Peel to finalise some financial affairs.'

'Yes,' she responded, dazed. 'But I never asked after him. I don't know what their conversations were. I only wanted to know what was necessary.'

Banner handed her a full tumbler. 'You were never curious to find out how he was holding out or if he ever had a message for you?'

'Thank you.' Patricia accepted the water and took a small sip. 'I told Naomi she should make it clear to him he didn't exist to me any more. She said he understood that. That he respected it.'

'So, she told you nothing.' Fabian wondered how to relay the conversation they'd had with Wisher's one-time lover.

'They had their own thing.' Patricia significantly held his eye. 'I knew Naomi had slept with him. Had been going to see him in prison before I asked her to.' But there was no other emotion on her face.

'Did you know about the affair at the time?'

She nodded once at his question. 'Chris told me. Confessed one bedtime. Said it had been eating him up.' Her voice was detached.

Fabian could only speculate how Wisher couldn't have been eaten up by the other things he'd been doing. 'How did you react?'

'In the time-honoured way – anger then eventual acceptance. We slept apart for one night but Liam was still at home so we carried on the pretence of normality until we'd worked things out.'

'And what about Naomi?'

'I never confronted her about it.'

'Why?' Banner asked, incredulously.

'She was one of the only friends I had. Her daughter played with my son. We were both lonely. The affair was over.'

'You believed that?' Fabian doubted she could so easily have forgiven her.

'Yes. Chris said he'd broken it off. I trusted him.'

'After he'd deceived you?' Banner sat down again.

'Our relationship after that was stronger than ever.' There was a flash of nostalgia in her dull brown eyes but it quickly vanished. 'Liam was having issues then. He needed both of us.'

'What sort of issues?' But Fabian already knew.

'A lot of things got on top of him.'

'You don't think he'd picked up on the tension between you and your husband?' Banner suggested.

'He was having difficulties at high school before then. He isolated himself from us. Spent a lot of time in his room.'

'Isn't that the usual behaviour of a teenager?'

Patricia tightened her lips at his comment. 'He was taking antidepressants. And he fought with me a lot. It was a volatile time.'

'Did Liam have an inkling about your husband?'

She shook her head at Fabian very deliberately. 'Neither of us knew, right up to you knocking on the door and him confessing.'

He could still vividly recall the day Wisher had sat down and reeled off the names of all his victims like a respectful roll call.

'You didn't harbour any doubts?' Fabian wondered if she'd been in denial. 'After all, he'd been having a secret affair with your ex-neighbour.'

'That was one of the reasons I remained friends with Naomi. I watched them both so closely after that. So closely that I didn't notice what else was going on.'

'When was the last time you saw Naomi Peel?' He'd already asked the other woman that question but wanted to make sure their stories tallied.

'September. She dropped off some papers that he'd signed to me.'

Banner checked her phone. 'Do you think she helped you out of guilt?'

'I don't know. I needed her, though. If there was still something between them I didn't care.'

'Not in the slightest?' Fabian watched for her reaction.

'Like I say, he doesn't exist.'

But he could see from her weary features that that was something she'd struggled to convince herself of. 'And Liam, how did he deal with what his father did?'

'You don't ever deal with it. And Liam was at a sensitive age. Way too young to be subjected to the glare of the media.' She fixed Fabian.

'We've spoken about this before, Patricia. When Angelina Friedmann started following me with her crew I hadn't been assigned the investigation.'

She nodded feebly. 'He's still struggling with it. Always will. Plus he's still fending off kids who only want to know him because of who his father was.'

Fabian leaned back in his chair. 'What about you? Have you been approached by anyone recently?'

'Not for some time. I don't think the cranks have tracked me here yet. But Liam still gets it a lot. There was a girl he was smitten with but it turned out she was more interested in Chris than him.'

'Would you mind if we spoke to him?'

Patricia looked at Fabian aghast. 'What for?'

'If he's being targeted by fanatics we need to know about them. What was this girl's name?'

She rolled her eyes up. 'Lindsay. Can't remember her surname. She was a couple of years older than Liam, I think.'

Banner pushed her purple specs further up her nose. 'How did he meet her, at college?'

'I was lucky to get her name. He doesn't tell me much. I do know he was really cut up when he ended it. That made it all about his father again. I guess he doesn't believe he's ever going to escape his shadow.'

Fabian was becoming more than familiar with people who wanted to touch those who had killed. 'Which college is he attending?'

'Bournemouth.'

'Would you mind giving us his number?' He expected a flat no. 'If it wasn't important I wouldn't ask.'

'You think the person who murdered those girls might have tried to make contact with him?'

'It's possible.' He waited as she gnawed her lip.

'Let me speak to him first.'

'Thank you. Will you be able to reach him now?'

Patricia raised her eyebrows at him in alarm.

'I'm sorry if I've got to push but we believe somebody else is about to be targeted.'

Patricia rose from her chair and went to the farmhouse dresser. She took her phone out of one of the drawers and dialled. She listened. 'I'm just getting his message.' She hung up.

Fabian got up. 'Any other number you can get him on?'

She shook her head.

He zipped up his leather jacket. 'What about email?'

'I can try but he never answers.'

Banner stood. 'Is he on WhatsApp, Facebook, Facetime?'

'If he is he hasn't included me.'

'Let us know as soon as you've spoken to him. Banner will give you her number.'

Banner did and took Patricia's and Liam's.

Patricia clasped her hands against herself. 'When I heard the news about Chris's suicide, I knew it wouldn't be over.'

Fabian thought she looked so lost. Would her life be forever tangled up with her husband's, even though his had now ended?

'They tell me we have to wait for the coroner's report before he can be cremated. More purgatory.'

Fabian didn't ask her the most obvious question.

'I've talked about it with Liam. Neither us will attend.'

Fabian nodded. 'Thanks for agreeing to see us. Please keep trying him.'

'Of course.'

'We'll see ourselves out.' Fabian made for the door and Banner followed.

They left Patricia dialling her son a second time. Outside in the garden the pile of leaves she'd blown off the lawn had been picked up by the wind and scattered all over it again.

CHAPTER TWENTY-FOUR

Just before midday Banner came out of the glass conference room and approached Fabian's desk holding her mobile. 'Heard from Patricia. She said Liam is standing by to talk to us.'

'Let's do it now.'

Banner nodded, speed dialled his number and handed her phone to him.

He stood, took it from her and held it to his ear as it rang.

'Hello?' a small, gruff voice said.

'Liam, I don't know if you remember me but it's Detective Inspector Fabian.'

'Yes?' he responded flatly.

'I'm sorry to intrude but I just need to ask you a few questions.'

'Mum explained.'

'OK. I was slightly concerned when she told us about some of the people who have been targeting you.' Fabian paced.

'It was just some of the kids in my class.'

'Your mother mentioned a girl named Lindsay.'

He sighed against the mouthpiece. 'We're not seeing each other any more.'

'I understand that. What was her surname?'

'Hewitt.'

'Did you meet her at college?'

'No.'

Fabian clenched his jaw when he said nothing else. 'Where then?'

'Just in a bar.'

'On campus?'

'No. In town.'

'Did she approach you?'

'Why?'

'It's important, Liam.'

'Yes.'

'Your mother tells me she was a few years older than you.'

'Yeah… a few years older.'

Fabian took a deep breath. 'So, how old?'

'Twenty-eight.'

'That's more than a few years.'

'I didn't want Mum to know. She would've only given me a hard time over it.'

'Maybe it's because your mother is looking out for your best interests.'

'Oh yeah, she's always been doing that,' Liam said contemptuously.

'So what happened with Lindsay?'

'We saw each other for a few months. She got me to open up, kept asking me about Dad. I felt duped so I dumped her…'

'What did she want to know?'

'Everything.'

'Specifically?'

'She was just a ghoul. It's been over since last year.'

'Do you still have a number for Lindsay?'

'Deleted her from my contacts.'

'Where does she live?'

'Rented a little flat in Springbourne but hadn't paid the rent there. Last I heard the landlord threw her out. Might have gone home to London now.'

'And you don't have those details?'

'No. Don't know anything about her family.'

'When did you last see her?'

'Like I say, it's over a year back.'

'And what about the other people your mother was telling us about? Were they all just people in college giving you a hard time?'

'Yeah. It stopped for a while but now the psychopath's topped himself it's started all over again.'

The term was an obvious indication as to how Liam characterised his father now. 'So nobody outside of class has communicated with you about him recently?'

'No,' he snapped. 'Except…'

Fabian waited and sensed Liam might be toying with him.

'…one guy called me. Said he was from a newspaper. Wanted to meet me for an interview. Said he'd pay me. I was tempted. I needed the cash. But I quickly came to my senses. Put the phone down on him.'

'What was his name?'

'Andrew something.'

'How long ago was that?'

'Couple of weeks. We used to get so many of them chasing us at home.'

'So how did he get hold of your number?'

There was a pause. 'He left a message for me to call him at the campus reception.'

'Have you still got it?'

'Doubt it.'

'And you can't recall his surname?'

'Sorry. It's probably not relevant anyway.'

'It may well be. Sure you can't remember?'

'He had an Irish accent. May have been an O at the start of his surname.'

Fabian was dubious. 'Which newspaper did he say he was from?'

'Not one that I'd heard of.'

'Local?'

'I don't know.' Liam retorted irritably.

'You've got our number now. If you remember any more details call us back. And think hard about anyone else who has approached you in the past few months you think might be suspicious.'

'OK. You think this copycat guy might try to contact my mother?'

Fabian thought he detected concern in his tone. 'You should both be wary.'

'Jesus, just when I thought I might be free of both of them.'

Fabian had to ask. 'Your mother just wants to protect you. What crime has she committed?'

'You'd better ask *her* that,' he said curtly.

'Liam, I don't have time for insinuations. I'd advise you not to withhold anything.'

'Don't worry, this is just about her exemplary mothering skills.'

'From my conversation with her today I know how much she cares about you.'

'Oh, she's very good at giving that impression.'

'Sounds like you two need to straighten some things out.'

'There's nothing straight about her.'

Fabian glimpsed his watch. 'Just ring us if you think of anything.' He hung up on Liam and turned to speak to Banner but she was standing on the far side of the office, her back to him, on her desk phone.

'Look, I've got to go,' she said in a low tone. 'I'll call you when I get a chance. Love you.' She replaced the handset and turned to him.

'OK?' he asked and held out her mobile before he saw the tear in her eye.

She nodded, appeared reluctant to approach him so he could see it.

'Liam Wisher says he hasn't seen his stalker girlfriend since last year.' Fabian put her phone on the desk and circled around it to sit so she could compose herself. Although he was tempted, Fabian was positive she wouldn't thank him for asking her about whatever she had going on the other end of the line. 'A guy who said he was a journalist tried to interview him recently, though.'

'Did he have a name for him?'

Fabian heard her approach his desk and took a sip of his fourth cup of coffee. 'Andrew something. Said he had an Irish surname. I'm not sure if Liam was tugging my chain, though.'

'Why would he do that?'

'Seems he's harbouring a grudge against Patricia and, I guess, anyone who's going to remind him of what his father did.' Fabian met her gaze as she sat on the edge of his desk and noticed she'd wiped away the tear.

'But if someone is obsessed with Wisher and his murders it's very likely they'd seek out his family.'

'Could have happened a long time ago, though. Patricia and Liam have had to fend off plenty of nutters. We don't have time to pursue everyone, particularly if Liam's details are sketchy.'

'So where to next?'

'I want to speak to the people who knew Wisher at Kerslake Prison. If the visitors' alibis all check out then as well as finding out who they're associating with we have to consider that there might be someone else on the inside acting as a go-between with whoever murdered our two victims.'

'A guard?'

'We need to know all the people he interacted with. Whether there were any other prisoners he had even a passing acquaintance with.'

Banner crossed her arms. 'But it looks like that list is pretty short.'

'Which means we should be able to put it together quickly.'

'So, who are we going to speak to? Briant may not be forthcoming if the reputation of Kerslake is on the line.'

'Someone I've wanted to speak to since my meeting with him.'

'Who?'

'Wisher's therapist, Christine Irvine. He beat her with his handcuffs in August of last year. She's at the prison this afternoon and has agreed to see me at three.'

Banner sniffed. 'So what do we do in the meantime?'

'You don't need to take care of anything?' Fabian nodded towards her desk phone.

'No. There's nothing I can do.' She bit her jaw.

'I don't want to pry but I can handle the Irvine interview if you'd rather be elsewhere.'

Banner seemed torn. 'No but I might need to step away at a moment's notice.' She swallowed.

Fabian knew she didn't want him to see how upset she was.

'Anything. Just tell me. Just tell me *when*, I mean.'

CHAPTER TWENTY-FIVE

Tilly came out of her Thursday lecture and the first thing she did was call Mark. She leaned on the sill in the corridor and looked out across the roofs to the study building he said he'd be in all day. He'd texted her myriad times in the last hour and had been making jokes about Dr Lockwood's halitosis, which he breathed all over her during the frequent occasions he lingered about her desk.

'You made it through without breathing apparatus?'

Tilly giggled. 'He circled me every time my phone buzzed thanks to you.'

'You shouldn't have been on your phone during class,' he mock chided her.

'So how come you were on yours?'

'I'm not in 'til this afternoon.'

'I thought you said you had lectures all day today.'

There was a brief pause. 'Morning was cancelled. Tiernan was sick.'

'So where are you now?'

'Back at the flat. Looking at the primordial soup that is last week's washing up.'

'Shame, I've got an hour at the library before my next lecture.'

'Hands full here. I don't even have rubber gloves.'

'Are you there on your own?'

Another pause. 'No, I've got help. It's not going to be pretty, though.'

'Who's there with you?'

'Jason.'

'Jason? Is he new? You haven't mentioned him before.'

'Sure I have,' he whispered. 'My flatmate. And I think he's earwigging our conversation.'

'How is his hygiene?'

'Entry level.'

Tilly smiled but was slightly irked. Did he really not want her to see where he was living? Surely it couldn't be that much of a hovel. Or did he just not want to subject her to the scrutiny of his flatmates?

'But he's more house trained than the others. That's why I've roped him in.'

Or maybe he was ashamed of her? He didn't seem keen on them hooking up with his friends or hers. Well, Ella, anyway. It had suited Tilly until now. She liked their intimate rendezvous. But it meant she'd spent all her evenings with him or listening to Ella arguing with her boyfriend on Facetime. Long distance relationships didn't appear to work but was Mark keeping her at arm's length? Was he even seeing someone else?

'We're going to try and separate the crockery but it all seems to be fused together with Thai green curry.'

Tilly told herself to calm down. If that was the situation then it was small wonder he was reluctant to have her visit. He'd told her his room had mildew and that there were things scuttling through the walls at night. It was probably an exaggeration but she knew he didn't have a lot of money. He'd said he'd applied late and that there were no spaces left on campus.

'You still there?'

'Yes.' She focussed on the conversation. 'Sounds like you have your work cut out.'

'We may discover some new bacteria cultures. Are you still on for tonight?'

'Yeah.' *Don't sound so keen, Tilly.*

'Did we say six for happy hour?'

'Think so.' *Keep the relief out of your voice.*

'McCools?'

He knew that. Was he just trying to be blasé? Weren't they past that? 'That's where you said.'

'Yeah. Just a minute,' he said away from the phone. 'Sorry, Till, duty calls.'

But Tilly was still troubled by the appearance of his new flatmate. She recalled the three other guys he lived with were Dan, Ed and Isaac. Surely there wasn't room for another. 'So, your helper?'

'Yeah?'

'Sorry, forgotten his name already.'

'Jason,' he said firmly.

Did he know she was testing him? What was she going to say: are you sure he is not a she? They hadn't even been dating a month. If she went possessive so early on she knew she'd frighten him away. *Keep it casual.* At least, let him think you are. 'Tell Jason to double-check your hazmat suit. I want you back in one piece.'

'I'll pass that on to my co-worker.' The good humour was back in his voice.

Had she just let him off the hook? 'I'd better leave you to whatever it is you're doing there then.' she added, just so he knew she had.

Was that suspicion in her voice? He couldn't afford to have her doubting him. 'If I get quarantined I'll let you know.' He looked down at the empty, padded metal chair before him. 'Sure you don't want to help out?' He cringed as he awaited her answer. If she only had an hour before her next lecture then she didn't have time to get into town and back. Would Tilly Fabian really skip a lecture for him? He needed her to believe that he was in his student flat in Beacon Heath.

'No, sounds like a two-man job.'

Was she still fishing? He couldn't put Jason on, he was fictional as were all his flatmates and he scolded himself for not keeping their names in his head. 'Shame, we need a hand harvesting the mushrooms from the walls as well.' He waited and was rewarded by a chuckle.

'So, no time for texting this afternoon?'

'I could send you a progress report.' He slowly paced around the tiny lock-up he was in. A strip light illuminated the grubby cinderblock walls and the only furniture on the cement floor was the chair and the small trolley bedside it.

'Maybe when you've carbon dated the curry.'

Good. She was participating again. 'How are you going to kill an hour?' He didn't want to give her the impression he wanted to get off the phone to avoid any more questions.

'Go to the library. Eat my lunch.'

'Don't eat too much. It's wings and nachos night at McCool's.'

'So you knew it was my birthday then?'

He paused, deliberately.

'Just kidding you.'

He sighed, audibly.

'It was yesterday.'

'Really?' But he knew it wasn't.

'No. It's September the 4th.'

'Cruel.' He gazed down at the implements on the trolley. 'Wait, does that mean you're a Virgo too?'

'Yes.' She sounded wary. As if he were trying to dupe her.

'I'm September the sixteenth.'

'Really?' But there was more hope in her voice than disbelief.

'Really.' He was Leo. 'Which makes me twelve days younger than you.'

'Toy boy,' she mocked.

But he could tell she was pleased with the revelation. 'Doesn't bother me, as long as you don't parade me around in front of your older friends.' Seemed like they were firmly back on track.

'Talking of friends, hadn't you better get back to yours?'

He noticed she did that often on the phone. Tried to round off the conversation before he did. Obviously she didn't want to appear too eager. He was relieved she didn't go through the whole 'you hang up first' routine, though. 'I'd better had.'

'Don't take any risks in there. That's why you have Jason.'

Hmmm. She still wasn't letting it go. He wasn't going to play along any more though. 'I'll see you tonight then.'

There was a gap. 'OK. You can tell me all about it then.'

'Come hungry.' He picked up the roll of black duct tape from the trolley.

'Wings and nachos? I'll probably leave hungry as well.'

'We can go somewhere else if you want.' He tried to sound hurt.

'And miss happy hour? You're buying the first round so don't be fashionably late.'

'OK.' He'd let her hang up.

'Enjoy!'

'I'll try to.'

She did.

He pocketed his phone and rubbed his face hard. He'd almost slipped up. Had to make sure he got his cast list straight in his head. He wouldn't have to for long but if he wanted to get Tilly Fabian into the chair he'd have to avoid making any more stupid mistakes.

He surveyed the apparatus on the trolley. Amongst the tools was a digital movie camera. He picked it up and fixed it onto the tripod he'd just erected when she'd called.

The other items lying on the trolley were favoured by his father and he had plenty of foil wrapped blades for the disposable scalpels. Everything was in place.

He turned off the light and locked up after himself, checking the padlock was tight before trudging back down the path through the forest and onto the derelict land at the rear of Goldbrook Farm.

He jumped into his Lexus, drove it through the gate then got back out and locked that securely. He slid into the driving seat again and headed to the ramp at the bottom of the track that dropped him onto the A379. Time to head back to town. It was half an hour away. He'd have plenty of time to get ready for his date with Tilly.

CHAPTER TWENTY-SIX

Doctor Christine Irvine's surgery had pale peach walls, dried flower arrangements and plush leather furniture.

'This is quite a contrast,' Fabian commented as she closed the door behind himself and Banner. Having made their way through the raucous, institutional corridors of the north wing of Kerslake Prison being greeted by such a pastel coloured and peaceful space was like stepping into an entirely different location.

She had no desk but instead headed towards a low leather chair at the rear of the room before turning and gesturing to the chaise longue opposite her. 'I do have a full schedule this afternoon.' Her voice was gentle and firm.

Fabian and Banner sat down and so did she.

'We appreciate you making the time.' He took in her stern expression and tried not to register how young he thought she looked. Late twenties? Her dyed blonde hair was pulled back severely from her slender face and secured by a black velvet band into a tight ponytail at the back of her head. Despite her attractive features she had grey bags under her blue eyes and he noted a purple scar under the make-up of her left cheekbone.

'Matt has explained the situation to me.'

First names terms with the governor? Fabian wondered if every member of staff was allowed to be as familiar. 'I gather you've been Wisher's therapist since he arrived at Kerslake.'

She nodded and her ponytail bounced.

'Were you aware of any other friendships he had here?'

She pursed her lips and shook her head at him. 'He didn't speak of any. But I only saw him once a month.'

'Not even the guards?'

'They were all… uneasy around him.'

'He wasn't an imposing man.'

'You interviewed him, Inspector. How did he make you feel?' She raised an eyebrow.

He indicated her scar. 'Was that a result of his assault?'

'No. That was another inmate. This was Chris.' She parted her blouse collar to reveal several dull red marks at the base of her throat. 'He punched me three times, used his cuffs as a knuckle duster.'

'Why?' Banner studied them, sickened.

'I'd just told him I'd turned him down as a potential candidate for Bicknell.'

'Was that the only time he was violent towards you?' Fabian looked up at her from the injury.

'Yes. I unlocked his cuffs in an early session. He always put them on the table while we talked.' Her gaze dropped to the piece of furniture between them.

'And, even after the attack, you continued assessing him?' Fabian was surprised she seemed so relaxed about the incident. 'Can't have been an easy decision.'

'It's not the worst that has been done to me,' she replied stoically.

'Why didn't you recommend him for Bicknell?' Fabian asked.

'He wouldn't have responded to their programme. It required him to show remorse and a willingness to rehabilitate.'

'Which he never did?'

'Only after I told him about the programme.'

'Did he tell you about the diary?' He watched her tuck a wisp of fair hair behind her ear.

'He told me he was keeping a journal but I never saw it.'

Banner put on her specs. 'Wouldn't his private thoughts have been more useful to you than him telling you what you wanted to hear?'

'Maybe so but it was his property,' Irvine answered simply.

'You said you weren't aware of any friendships with other inmates but what was his conduct like with them? Any violence?'

She shook her head at Fabian. 'No, but I understand he got into an altercation with a prisoner in the canteen some time ago.'

'A physical fight?'

'No. A verbal one. Matt told me about it after Chris attacked me. Apparently he had most of his meals in his cell after that.'

Fabian had thought Wisher had confined himself to his cell from day one. 'Can you remember how long ago and who the inmate was?'

'A year and a half maybe. Don't think it would have justified logging the incident, though. The other prisoner was Doug Compton.'

'Is he still serving time at Kerslake?' Banner got out her phone to access her notebook.

'Yes. Aggravated assault. I saw him a couple of weeks ago.'

Fabian exhaled. 'So Wisher would have been having his meals in the canteen up until then?'

'I assume so.'

That meant Wisher was rubbing shoulders with the other inmates for a year and a half before. Naomi Peel had led Fabian to believe he'd taken all his meals in his cell. Where would they even start? 'Were you taken aback by his suicide?'

She pondered the question for a few moments. 'Yes.'

'You had to think about that,' Fabian observed.

'We'd spoken about suicide.'

'Wisher threatened it?' He noticed her shift uncomfortably for the first time.

'No. We discussed the mechanics. He was curious as to what was the most popular method.'

'Sounds like Kerslake has had its fair share.'

'No more than other institutions.'

'That's not what the stats say,' Banner interjected.

Irvine looked sharply at her. 'We have an overcrowding issue.'

Fabian could see it was a sensitive subject. 'Did you get the impression Wisher was contemplating suicide?'

'No. If I had I wouldn't have entertained the conversation. Wisher said he found the idea of suicide reprehensible and that it was only acceptable if it had meaning for others.'

Fabian considered what Wisher hanging himself had initiated. 'And do you think he changed his mind when he had his cancer diagnosis?'

'He was able to divert himself when he was alone. He read voraciously. I think the idea of him losing his mental faculties must have been terrifying.'

Fabian changed tack. 'Where was he examined?'

'Frithfield Hospital.'

'Who was his oncologist?'

'Doctor Patlow.'

Banner made notes.

Fabian paused for her to finish. 'Did he discuss his family with you?'

'No. I think he'd resigned himself to the fact that he wouldn't see them again.'

Banner sat forward. 'Did he talk about the people who came to visit him?'

Irvine didn't turn to her when she answered. 'Not much. He mentioned one woman. Said she was obsessed with him.'

'Jennifer Keene?' she asked.

'No. Naomi...'

'Peel?' Fabian was puzzled he hadn't mentioned his stalker. 'What did he say about her?'

'That she fulfilled him sexually.'

Fabian frowned. 'How?'

'In his mind, of course.'

'You assume?'

'It couldn't have been any other way.' Her reply to him dried and she coughed.

He allowed her to finish clearing her throat. 'Because his visits were always supervised?'

'Yes. The procedures here are rigorous.'

Same answer as Briant had given him. 'We've learned that Ms Peel was acting as his wife's representative…'

'I don't know about that but he said the memory of his infidelity with her replaced the relationship he no longer had with Patricia.' Irvine glanced at her watch.

Fabian let her eyes to return to his. 'And how was *your* relationship with him?'

'He was placid except for that one occasion.'

He detected a twitch at the left corner of her mouth. 'Did he show remorse for attacking you?'

'No. He didn't even mention it the next time I saw him.'

'You must have been nervous to see him again.' There was sympathy in Banner's voice.

Irvine still didn't look at her. 'It was like it had never happened. He behaved as he had prior to the attack.'

'And how was that?' Fabian could see her shoulders loosen.

'Courteous, respectful.'

Even though she'd been dismissive before, Fabian got the impression the doctor was glad to have moved beyond the questions about the attack. 'I interviewed him for three straight weeks and found he had a way of making me feel we were close friends.

Even during my brief, recent conversation with him here. Is that something that happened to you?'

Irvine shrugged. 'A lot of prisoners try to ingratiate themselves.'

'But specifically Wisher. He didn't instil that feeling in you?'

'No,' she replied flatly. 'As for your experience you have to remember that Wisher held you in very high regard.'

'So I believe.' Fabian tried not to look as uncomfortable with that as he felt. 'Why do you think that was the case?'

'He told me. You were responsible for his capture. You stopped him.'

'And that's what he wanted all along? For me to intervene?'

'He didn't appear to resent you for it. But I don't believe the truth was something he was generous with. Not with me anyway.' Her expression hardened.

'Because he was saying what you wanted to hear so he could get into Bicknell?'

She nodded at him. 'For the main part.'

'So did Matt—' Fabian deliberately corrected himself 'Governor Briant have much contact with Wisher?'

'He sat in on the reviews. Other than that I don't think so.'

'Not even after the attack?'

'I was in the hospital, I don't know what happened here during my recuperation period.'

'Was there punishment for Wisher? Solitary? Loss of privileges?' Banner asked.

'I don't know.'

Fabian exchanged a look with Banner. 'And how long did it take you to recover?'

'Only a few weeks.'

He scratched his chin. 'Did you have any therapy?'

She shook her head. 'It wasn't the first incident and it probably won't be the last.'

'What *did* you learn about him?' Again he waited as she formulated a response.

'He was manipulative. I don't think anyone ever saw the real Chris. Not even his wife.' She got abruptly to her feet. 'Now, I really have to see my next patient or I'll be swamped.'

Fabian stood too.

Banner followed. 'Naomi Peel? Do you think *she* knew him?'

Irvine haughtily regarded her. 'You'd have to ask her that.' She returned her attention to Fabian. 'Was there anything else?'

'Not for the moment. Thanks for giving up your time. We'll be back in touch if we need anything more from you.'

Irvine wordlessly held the door open and closed it behind them.

'She seemed a little precious,' Banner whispered as they made their way back down the now silent corridor of the north wing.

'Perhaps she sees his death as a personal failing.' But Fabian was positive she'd been concealing something.

'Surely she would have known if Wisher had been punished for the attack. And she was pretty spiky with me.'

'Maybe she didn't like you pointing up the fact that Kerslake has such poor suicide stats.'

Banner didn't look convinced. 'I think there was more between them than a doctor–patient relationship.'

Doctor Irvine seems to be on first name terms with the governor too.'

'I noticed that.'

'And I think Briant was more than happy with Irvine's assessment of Wisher in terms of Bicknell.' Fabian hooded his eyes.

'What are you saying?'

'Perhaps there's another reason why Wisher was refused, other than his unsuitability.'

'Like what?'

'He was a high-profile prisoner. Maybe Briant didn't want to lose him to a more progressive institution.'

Banner considered this as a guard unlocked the first barred door they had to pass through.

'He'd also read Wisher's diary prior to his death.' Fabian lowered his voice as they did.

'And?'

'Why would he have it? I don't think Wisher would have willingly given it up, especially as it was intended as instructions for whoever he has on the outside.'

'So, Briant confiscated it?'

'Maybe.'

Fabian looked back at the guard as he sealed the door behind them. He recognised him as the one he'd spoken to about Wisher on his last visit and nodded to him before turning and continuing down the corridor. 'We should speak to Briant while we're here.' Fabian checked his watch. 'Let's try his office and see if he's in.'

CHAPTER TWENTY-SEVEN

'Sorry for barging in on your day. This is Detective Sergeant Banner.'

'You really should have phoned ahead.' Briant stood back from the door he'd just opened to them. 'I have appointments in the city. Will this take long?'

'We've just had a conversation with Doctor Irvine.'

'Yes.' Briant nodded impatiently at Fabian; he clearly knew about the interview. He seated himself behind his desk and gestured for them to sit in the two chairs before it.

Fabian sat the same time as Banner and wondered if Briant had actually just been on the phone to Doctor Irvine. 'You know her well?'

'What do you mean?' Briant seemed immediately defensive.

'I'm just saying, if she's been working here for...'

Briant rolled his eyes upward, as if struggling to remember. 'Just over three years I think.'

Fabian knew it was a performance. 'And you helped her through the difficult time after Wisher attacked her in the surgery...'

'Yes?' Briant seemed wary of the line of questioning. 'Any employer would.'

Fabian thought he was definitely concealing a relationship with Doctor Irvine. 'We were just wondering what happened to Wisher in terms of being disciplined after the event?'

Briant's frame relaxed a little. 'I suspended his library visits. That was the one thing I knew he valued.'

'Was that sufficient?' Banner crossed her leg.

Briant looked at Fabian and Fabian nodded that he had to answer her. 'I deemed it so.'

'And what was his response?' Fabian continued.

'He accepted it without complaint.'

'You told him yourself?'

'Yes. What he did was vicious. It could have been far worse though.'

'You punished him less because he didn't *kill* Doctor Irvine?' Banner said deadpan.

'No. Of course not.'

'How often did you speak with him?'

Briant checked himself before replying to Fabian. 'I don't recall. I was present at his reviews and I would have seen him when I conducted my inspections.'

'Did you often speak directly with him, though?' he pushed.

'From time to time.'

'What was the nature of the conversations outside of assessments for Bicknell?'

Briant puffed his cheeks and sighed as if he were already bored with Fabian's questions. 'They would have been perfunctory conversations about his conditions.'

'So how did his diary come into your hands?'

'I told you. I read it when he made the request to give it to you.'

'So you read it, what, the day before?'

Briant blinked rapidly at him.

'You'd clearly read the whole thing when I first visited.'

'It was probably a couple of days before. Yes, he made the request and I asked to read it. Why are you grilling me like this?'

'I just want to establish exactly whose hands the diary passed through before it came to me. Did he give it to you personally?'

'No.'

Fabian waited for him to expand on that but he didn't. 'Who brought it to you then?'

'One of the guards.'

'Which one?'

'Barclay.' Briant didn't need to think about that. 'Keith Barclay.'

Banner took out her phone and tapped her notebook. 'Is he on duty at the moment?'

'I can find out. But I'm already running late.'

'I won't detain you any longer than necessary,' Fabian assured him. 'Did Wisher have a problem with you examining the diary?'

'No, he said he understood it was procedure and that there was nothing in it he'd have a problem with me reading.'

Wisher was no longer alive to dispute that. 'So you had a direct conversation with him about it?'

Briant swivelled in his chair a few times. 'Yes.'

'Did you tell Doctor Irvine about the diary?'

'I don't recall.'

Fabian could see he was being deliberately vague in case she'd said otherwise. 'Surely you remember.'

'I probably did. Look, I have three hundred other inmates to consider.'

'But none like Wisher,' Banner retorted.

Briant held up his hands. 'It may have been me. Perhaps at lunch.'

'So you see her—'

Briant cut Banner off. 'From time to time.'

Fabian let him take a breath. 'How long did you know about the diary?'

'I knew he was working on something but only found out that it was a diary when he requested he be able to hand it to you.'

'So nobody else except you and Barclay would have seen it?'

'There are a number of guards who work his block but, from what I understand, nobody wanted to interact with Wisher.'

'How can you be sure?'

'Ask Michaels. He's the senior officer on east wing.'

'Could we speak with him as well?' Fabian looked at the phone on Briant's desk.

'Now?'

He nodded at Briant. 'Before you dash off.'

Briant picked up the receiver as if it were a dead animal and dialled. 'Jill, can you get Geoff Michaels on the phone as soon as possible. Thank you.' He replaced it.

'And the attack on Doctor Irvine, it was Wisher's reaction to being turned down for Bicknell?'

Briant looked at him askance. 'Yes. I thought you'd just spoken to Doctor Irvine.'

'We have. I just wondered if you talked to Wisher directly after the event and if he confirmed his motive to you.'

'I did and he more or less acted as if it had never happened.'

Which confirmed Irvine's version of events. 'Did you want Doctor Irvine to continue treating Wisher?' Fabian watched his reaction closely.

Briant inhaled. 'I told her she didn't have to.'

Fabian could see that he was genuinely distressed by her decision. 'But she ignored your advice?'

'She said it would be beneficial to both of them.'

Fabian understood that. 'Still, it was a brave choice.'

'She's been attacked by inmates before.'

But Fabian could tell that that was no comfort to him. 'And there were no incidents with Wisher following that one?'

'No. Not that I'm aware of,' he added quickly. The desk phone bleeped and Briant seemed glad of the interruption. He picked up. 'Thanks, Jill. Michaels, can you spare some time to talk to some police officers about Christopher Wisher? Your office? And they'd like to speak with Barclay as well… Thanks.' He put down the receiver and addressed Fabian. 'You can find his office on the first floor of east wing but I really have to fly now.' He stood and moved some papers around his desk.

They both got to their feet.

Fabian walked to the door but paused. 'One more thing before we go…'

Briant inhaled again and was clearly eager to leave.

'Who found Wisher's body?'

'That was Barclay too.'

'Must have been very disturbing for him.'

'I *did* ask him to submit to our therapy package…'

'And he's turned it down?'

'Yes. Didn't even want to take any leave. A good thing really, we're understaffed as it is.'

'So he's been on duty every day since?'

'Yes,' Briant answered Fabian tersely.

CHAPTER TWENTY-EIGHT

As Fabian and Banner climbed the stairs to Michaels's office the low murmur emanating from behind the sealed grey door suddenly stopped. Fabian bounced his eyebrows at Banner and rapped his knuckles on the panel.

'Yes?' a deep male voice said, as if surprised by their arrival.

Fabian turned the handle, entered and found two uniformed officers in the room, which reeked of sweat and was about a quarter of the size of Briant's office. The older, bald and paunchier officer was seated on the edge of his desk with his arms folded. Fabian estimated him to be in his fifties, he had a bushy ginger beard and regarded them through half closed eyes. The other stocky and square-jawed younger officer wore his hat and a slightly nervous expression.

Fabian introduced themselves and wondered what confab he'd just interrupted. 'Thanks for giving up your time.'

Michaels jerked his thumb. 'This is Officer Barclay.'

The younger man hovered awkwardly.

Fabian noted the brown bruise over Barclay's eye. There were no other chairs so he closed the door to give them room. 'We've just interviewed Doctor Irvine and your governor. He tells me you both had contact with Christopher Wisher.'

Barclay turned to Michaels and waited for him to answer first.

'I largely dealt with him,' was all he offered.

'Wasn't it you who found him, though?' Fabian fixed Barclay. He nodded once.

Banner kept her tone casual. 'Was he acting strangely at all that night?'

Barclay looked as if the questioning was already more than he expected. He shot a look at Michaels again.

'The other officers avoided speaking to him if they could.'

'Maybe Officer Barclay can answer the question,' Fabian insisted. 'Is that right?'

Barclay nodded again. 'Yes. Wisher put everyone on edge.'

'How so?' But Fabian understood.

'He studied everyone. And said little. It was unnerving.' Barclay wrung one hand with the other.

'So how did you react when you found him hanging in his cell?'

'I threw up.' Barclay stared at the wall as if Wisher were dangling there. 'His face was dark blue and his eyes looked like they were on the brink of popping out of his head.'

'Have you ever found another inmate like that?' Banner inquired gently.

'It was his first,' Michaels answered for him.

'So you've not worked here long then?' Fabian calculated him to be in his mid-twenties.

'Nearly two years,' he replied, slightly affronted.

'And it was really your first?' Fabian saw hostility wash over Michaels's face.

'Yep.' Barclay's features hardened as well.

'Nasty bruise,' Banner declared, indicating her own brow for reference.

'Nasty job,' Michaels countered.

'So how do you think Wisher got hold of the carpet tie he hanged himself with?' Fabian directed the question at the senior officer.

Michaels sniffed and kept his arms crossed. 'He could have been given it by another inmate.'

'But I didn't think Wisher socialised with the other inmates, particularly after a disagreement with one in the canteen. Who was that with?' Fabian already knew the answer.

'Douglas Compton,' Michaels said bluntly.

That corroborated Irvine's story. 'Where else could he have got it, d'you think?'

Michaels blinked at Fabian a few times, clearly displeased with his insinuation. 'He could have been given the carpet tie some time ago and been hiding it for the right occasion.'

'And how was your relationship with him?'

Michaels swung his pale blue eyes to Banner. '"Relationship?"' he repeated sardonically. 'I kept my exchanges with Wisher to a minimum, like everyone else.'

'And what about the relationship between the governor and Doctor Irvine?'

Michaels responded to Fabian's question with a deep frown.

'I've spoken to them both now. Let's not pretend it's a secret.'

'It's their business,' Michaels stated dismissively.

Fabian noticed Barclay's eyes were now fixed to the floor. 'I know Briant was angry about the attack on Doctor Irvine.'

The senior officer sucked on his bottom lip. 'You'll have to speak to him about that.'

'We have, I just wanted to find out what you know about it.'

Michaels shrugged at Fabian. 'I just said, their business.'

'You got the diary from Wisher and took it to the governor, didn't you?'

Barclay looked up at Fabian. 'He asked me to.'

'Yes, he told me that. What day was that?'

Barclay squinted.

'Day before Wisher committed suicide?' Fabian thought Briant had seemed cagey when he'd been questioned about how long he'd had the diary.

'It was at least a week before that.' Barclay then clammed shut, as if he was afraid he'd said the wrong thing.

Banner didn't give him time to think. 'Did you examine the diary?'

'Oh no,' Barclay said, categorically.

'Not even a little curious?' Fabian narrowed his eyes conspiratorially. 'I probably would have been.'

Barclay's gaze was solid. 'No.'

'OK.' But Fabian doubted it. 'So you took the diary directly to the governor?'

Barclay's stare weakened. 'Uh…' He looked at Michaels.

'Tell him exactly what happened,' the senior officer said, matter-of-factly.

But Barclay looked even more nervous. 'I gave it to Officer Michaels.'

Fabian's attention shifted to him. 'Why was that?'

'I asked him to bring it to the office. I didn't trust Wisher so I wanted to check it over before it left the wing.'

'What did you think you'd find?' Banner demanded first.

Michaels still kept his arms knotted. 'He's devious. I wanted to be thorough.'

'Had you experienced him being devious then?' Fabian watched him chew his beard for a few seconds.

'I knew how he'd duped Doctor Irvine. I told her she shouldn't take his cuffs off.'

Fabian could see his cheeks starting to flush. 'So you were upset by what happened to Doctor Irvine?'

'Of course. We all were,' he added quickly.

It looked to Fabian as if Doctor Irvine had more than one admirer, but he kept to the point. 'And did your handling of Wisher change after the attack?'

Michaels frowned. 'What are you saying?'

'It would be understandable.'

'Are you saying I put the carpet tie around his neck?' Michaels stood from the edge of the desk.

'No. Wisher wrote down the date of his own death. I just wonder if he had some help getting hold of what he needed to do it.'

'I wish I *had* been part of it.' Michaels knew the gravity of what he was saying. 'After what he did to the people he murdered and to Doctor Irvine I really do. But that was something that took all of us by surprise.'

Fabian quickly checked Barclay. He was staring at the floor again. 'So how long was the diary in your possession?'

'A couple of hours. Barclay gave it to me just before lunch. I checked it over after.'

'So you read it?'

'A lot of rambling. Couldn't see why anyone would want to read it.'

'Except the governor,' Fabian reminded him.

Michaels shrugged. 'I suppose he had to.'

'Because there might have been something that put Kerslake in a bad light?' Banner prompted.

Michaels sighed. 'So, are my staff on trial here?'

Fabian could see Banner had hit a nerve. 'I know the governor is eager to restore Kerslake's reputation.'

Michaels's complexion flushed further. 'Have you any idea what we have to contend with every day? You guys catch them, you don't have to fucking wet-nurse them.'

Fabian held up a placatory hand. 'What happened then? You gave the diary back to Officer Barclay…'

'I gave the diary back to Officer Barclay and he took it directly to the governor.'

'Directly?'

Barclay nodded at Fabian.

'And nobody else saw it?' He could see neither of them could attest to that.

'Not that I'm aware of,' Michaels enunciated each word.

'OK. Thank you, both. Can you tell me which wing Douglas Compton is on?'

'He's with us.' Michaels unfolded his arms but didn't seem any less combative.

'Is there any chance we could speak with him before we leave?' Fabian suspected Michaels wasn't going to be jumping to do him any favours now.

Michaels ran his tongue around his mouth. 'We'll bring him to the visitors' room, although he doesn't like police officers.'

'Who here does?' Fabian wondered if Michaels caught the irony.

'No. He *really* doesn't like police officers.'

CHAPTER TWENTY-NINE

Fabian and Banner made their way to the visitors' room. It was the same one he'd had his last meeting with Wisher in. He went to the exact table and sat down. Was this where the serial killer had passed instructions to Ainsley Naylor, Jennifer Keene, Ronan Fuller or Naomi Peel? According to the records Wisher had no other visitors since his arrival at Kerslake.

His phone buzzed and he opened the text message he'd just received.

We need to talk.

It was from Angelina Friedmann. He hadn't heard from her since Wisher's trial. From what he'd gathered, her career path had been stratospheric but after his management's hostility towards him because of what they perceived as his over-reliance on the media, he'd kept his distance. Holding one of the top editorial positions at *News 24* probably meant Angelina was under even more pressure to deliver the goods, however, even if she would be doing more delegating than journalistic legwork.

Banner was on the other side of the room having a low conversation on her phone with her back to him. He assumed she was snatching a moment to deal with whatever situation she had at home so swiftly replied:

No time. Maybe when dust settles.

His phone immediately vibrated again.

Think we have a mutual interest. Wisher's not going away.

Did Friedmann already know the specifics of Nadine James or Polly O'Rourke's murders? He didn't doubt she had someone feeding her information from Horseferry but if she blew the lid on what was going on he knew who Metcalfe would blame for the leak.

Don't jump to any conclusions. Hold fire. Will call later.

He counted the seconds before she responded and reached three.

Will wait an hour.

It was an implicit threat.

'Halt there.' The guard didn't bark the order, though.

Fabian registered it was Barclay. His attention then shifted to the tall forty-something man filling the gated doorway to the visitors' room. His head looked a little too small for the broad body below it, particularly as a hairnet contained his short fair curls. There obviously wasn't a size of jade green overalls big enough for him and the contours of his muscles stretched the material tight around his frame.

Barclay unlocked and opened the door but didn't order him inside.

Fabian guessed he was as intimidated by Compton as he felt himself.

Banner finished her call and came to sit next to Fabian as Compton strolled stiffly over. His hands were in cuffs but Fabian got the impression they wouldn't really be an impediment if he decided to let off steam. There was no skin visible on his arms. They were black, blue and green with badly drawn tattoos.

Fabian waited for his squeaking trainers to reach the table. 'Mr Compton, thanks for giving up your time.'

Barclay pulled the door closed and locked it.

'You're lucky I was on canteen duty.' Compton sniffed in harshly through his swollen nose as if he were about to spit. 'I'd rather do anything than dole out that shit. Even talk to coppers.' He sat rigidly and the plastic chair creaked against its metal legs.

Fabian didn't bother with introductions. He and Banner weren't even humans in Compton's eyes.

'If it's about a deal you're wasting your time, though.'

'No. We just want to ask you about Christopher Wisher.' Fabian watched the satisfaction settle on his face.

'I don't like to speak ill of the dead.'

'You had a run-in with Wisher some time ago,' Fabian began, deciding that if Compton was just going to wind him up he would quickly suspend the conversation. Michaels had told him about his reason for being inside. He'd put a policewoman in a wheelchair after attacking her with an iron post.

'You seem to know all about it already.'

'Can you remember what it was about?' Banner asked casually.

He contemplated her and the shadow of something indecent immediately swooped across his expression. 'We were having a disagreement.'

'About?' she asked, as he wanted her to.

'About whether female pigs were easier to kill than male pigs.'

'Which side of the fence were you on?' she immediately rejoined, undeterred.

'I wasn't on any side of the fence. I always like to get in the sty and find out for myself. They certainly squeal a lot more, though.'

'OK, he's ready to go back to his canteen shift,' Fabian said to Barclay.

Compton fixed him, gauging whether he was bluffing.

Fabian rose from his chair and addressed Banner. 'We don't have time for this.'

Banner got to her feet too.

'Wait.' Compton theatrically pouted. 'I've only just got down here.'

Fabian zipped up his leather jacket. 'I understand you're up in front of the parole board in eight weeks' time. I'm really not sure if this constitutes good behaviour, though.'

Compton's face didn't alter.

'Your call.' Fabian nodded to their exit. 'I have to speak to Briant on the way out. Wisher died in here. Perhaps you're determined to as well.'

Compton was still impassive but he held up his palm.

Fabian paused. 'Do we need to sit again?'

Compton silently sucked his lips. 'He asked me about my drone boy.'

Fabian remained standing. 'You had a delivery service?' Michaels had told him that Compton had been caught dealing. He'd heard the stories of prisoners smuggling in drugs and phones by having them flown by drones and dropped at strategic windows.

'Did have, 'til they put screens on all the windows. Now it's back to more traditional methods. For the others I mean. I steer clear now.' Compton chewed at the side of his thumbnail.

'Of course you do. What did he want brought in. Or taken out?'

'What's this all about? You think somebody put that noose around his neck?'

'Just answer the questions. Did he want you to smuggle something for him?'

Compton nibbled skin for a while before he answered. 'Conversation didn't get that far.'

'Had you spoken to him before then?'

Compton shook his head once, as if the gesture was better than actually conversing with Fabian.

'Were you afraid of him?' Banner sat back down.

He eyeballed her with the same lewd intent. As if memorising every inch of her. 'Yeah, course I was.' He breathed in, puffed out his chest.

Fabian joined her. 'He approached you in the canteen, you turned him down. How did it turn into a shouting match?'

'Who said it did?' Compton examined his thumb.

'We've been reliably informed. So what happened?'

Compton shrugged. 'He wouldn't let it go.'

Fabian could see the raw, red skin exposed on the side of his thumb. 'You weren't curious as to why he wanted to use the drone?'

'No. Wisher was a creepy fuck. I wanted him as far away from me as possible.'

'Because of what you knew about his crimes?' But Fabian sensed there was something else.

'No because of how he'd turned Singleton.'

That was a name Briant hadn't mentioned to Fabian. 'Another inmate?'

'Friend of mine 'til Wisher took his tray over to his table.'

Fabian wondered how much of a friend. From what Michaels had told them Compton liked the younger inmates.

Compton hissed through his broken nose. 'Don't know what he filled his head with but there were rumours about them.'

Fabian prompted. 'Sexual rumours?'

'Don't think they ever got the opportunity but Singleton definitely only had eyes for Wisher.'

'What's Singleton in for?'

'Was in for. He's out now.'

Fabian swapped a look with Banner. 'How long ago?'

'End of 2017. Good behaviour. You really don't know Leighton Singleton?' He regarded them both with disdain.

But that suddenly rang a vague bell with Fabian.

'I ain't saying nothing more. Go and do your job. When Singleton was released that's when Wisher starts sniffing around me. I wasn't having the same things said about me. I told him I'd panel him if I saw him in the canteen again.'

Fabian knew there had been no record of a Leighton Singleton visiting Wisher. 'Did anybody else inside want Wisher dead?'

'I told you, that's all I know.' Compton folded his arms.

It reminded Fabian of Michaels.

He lowered his voice. 'If you're scared of Briant finding out—'

Compton shot a glance back at Barclay. 'I ain't scared of Briant. I just know I'm not about to fuck up my review. I've said as much as I'm going to. Singleton was the only one who spent any time with Wisher. Talk to him. Can I go now?'

'But you've only just got down here.' Fabian fed his own line back to him.

'I've helped you. If you make things hard for me with Briant you'll be finding out who *I* know on the outside.'

Banner was as unfazed as Fabian. 'I take it that's a promise not a threat.'

'It's been a pleasure meeting you both. Keith, I'm ready to leave now.'

Barclay unlocked the door to the visitors' room.

Fabian turned to Banner. 'Isn't it nice that everyone here is on first name terms.'

Compton got to his feet, turned on his heels and squeaked out without saying another word.

CHAPTER THIRTY

As they made their way across the prison car park to Fabian's green Audi, the low, grubby afternoon smog clouds cast an eerie yellow light. Banner hung up the call she'd made to Horseferry Station. 'Finch says Leighton Singleton is in organised crime.'

He knew he'd recognised the name.

'One of the heavies for the Prentice family.'

Fabian was more than familiar with them. Based in south-west London their front was property repossessions but extortion was their real bread and butter. 'Odd that someone like Wisher would involve himself with Singleton.'

'Perhaps for protection.'

'Or because Singleton was getting out.'

Banner's phone beeped.

'That an address for him?'

She squinted at her screen. 'Croydon.'

Fabian unlocked the Audi with his remote key. 'We'll head over there now.'

'You feeling as if we're only getting half the picture back there?'

He opened his door. 'If Briant is lying about his relationship with Christine Irvine, what else is he hiding?'

She opened hers and got in the vehicle. 'Briant wears a wedding ring. Perhaps he's just like any other married man who doesn't want to get found out.'

Fabian slid into the driving seat. 'Maybe but why did he have Wisher's diary for almost a week before letting him hand it to me?'

'Perhaps it was lying in his in-tray for a while before he got round to it.'

He slid on his seatbelt. 'No. I think he's paranoid about Kerslake getting any more bad press. I imagine it was priority.'

'So he took his time.' Banner put on hers. 'Made doubly sure there was nothing incriminating in there before contacting you.'

'But why lie about the time he had it?'

Banner nodded thoughtfully. 'Michaels and Barclay seemed very edgy too.'

'Suffering from the same, you think? In that environment, they must all be petrified of putting a foot wrong.' He started the engine.

'I think Barclay was being given a hasty pep talk when we arrived at Michaels's office.'

Fabian pulled them out of the space. 'He was definitely taking his cues from Michaels.'

'Another thing. Can we trust what Compton told us?'

'We follow up. With his review pending he'd be foolish to send us down any obvious dead ends.'

'But prisoners like Compton can't help themselves.'

Fabian accelerated to the exit. 'After Singleton was released Wisher was obviously trying to find a way of communicating with people outside the prison.'

'*Then* he was. Perhaps he found a sympathetic ear inside.'

'Who? Back to Doctor Irvine?'

'She was definitely withholding.'

'Yes. More than an obvious fascination with Wisher as a subject, though?' He passed through the gate as it slid open and dropped down the ramp.

'Maybe Wisher's attack on her was nothing to do with his recommendation for Bicknell. She seemed sensitive about Naomi Peel.'

'Why d'you think that was?'

'Jealousy?'

He turned right onto the road around the long curved wall of the prison. 'If there was something between them, why did he assault her?'

'Whatever the cause, she still wanted to go on treating him.'

'She's been attacked before. Episodes like that are part of her job.'

'And why did Briant go so easy on Wisher? Removal of library privileges?' she said caustically.

'Could have been Irvine's intervention if it was counterproductive to her therapy for Wisher.'

Banner punched the postcode from her phone into Fabian's satnav. 'Or because Briant wanted to give Wisher as easy a time as he'd have in Bicknell. He was his most high profile inmate.'

'Kudos for Kerslake.' Fabian agreed. 'And if he had the ear of Doctor Irvine…'

Banner raised her eyebrows. 'They could keep him there indefinitely. Whether Wisher was willing or not.'

CHAPTER THIRTY-ONE

Fabian and Banner arrived at Leighton Singleton's address just as it was getting dark. Otterburn Street was a narrow road with barely enough room to manoeuvre the car because of the vehicles parked on both sides.

'Seventeen A, this is it.' Banner indicated the house to their right. It had a tiny front garden that was stacked with black refuse sacks. The window on the first floor had an illuminated yellowing net in it. 'Singleton has rented here ever since being released from Kerslake.'

Fabian pulled over as near as possible and switched off the Audi's engine. They both got out.

There were bells for two flats so Fabian hit Singleton's, which was on the first floor. No reply. He rapped the knocker. And then again.

They heard rustling from within before the door opened. A stocky, unshaven man in his late twenties with a grubby white towelling robe that was too small for him was standing there in a pair of black flip-flops. His straggles of dark hair were plastered to his scalp and he'd clearly just got out of the shower. His face dropped, as if he'd been expecting someone else.

'Mr Singleton?'

'No.' He shook his head at Fabian. 'He lives in the upstairs flat.'

'I'm sorry. I rang his bell.' Fabian knew he was talking to Singleton, though. Banner had shown him an image.

'He's not in. You can leave a message with me though, if you like.'

'Mind if we come in?' Banner guessed Fabian was playing along.

Singleton blocked the doorway with his body. 'What for?'

'Police.' Fabian showed him his ID and watched Singleton tense. 'Mind if we ask you a few questions about him?'

Singleton didn't even look at the ID. 'Whatever. I don't know him that well, though. He's hardly ever here.' He stepped back to allow them entry.

Fabian and Banner squeezed into the tiny hallway.

'Fire away then.' He examined the grubby scarlet carpet.

'It's a little cramped here. Can't we go inside your flat?' Fabian gestured to the front door behind Singleton, which he assumed he didn't have a key for.

'It's a mess. In the middle of decorating at the moment.'

'You can cut the act, we know you're Singleton.' He nodded at the stairs. 'Shall we?'

Singleton opened his mouth to protest but thought better of it.

Fabian put away his ID. 'Why the lies?'

'I thought the landlord might have sent you.' But Singleton had to think about the excuse.

'After you then.' Fabian swept a palm to the steep flight of stairs carpeted in the same colour as the hallway.

Singleton turned and trudged heavily up them. Fabian and Banner went up close behind him. They passed a bathroom with the shower over the bath still dripping. A green waterproof curtain mottled by mould had been drawn back beside it.

Singleton pushed open the door ahead of them and they followed him into a small room that was mostly taken up by a large double bed. Beside it was a stand containing a microwave, toaster and kettle. On a shelf beside the window the TV was switched onto the news.

The room smelt of mildew and deodorant and Fabian noted the laptop that was open on the bed.

Singleton quickly closed the lid and turned to them. 'Well, you asked to come in here. Make it quick.'

'Got somewhere you need to be?' Banner asked.

Singleton pulled the robe tighter around him. 'Yeah, as a matter of fact.'

'Where?' Fabian confirmed they were now blocking the only exit out of the room. 'Busting down doors for the Prentice family tonight?'

'They're a legit enforcement agency.'

'I don't want to talk about them. Not this time anyway.'

Singleton scowled at him. 'What then?'

'Christopher Wisher.' Fabian saw the name briefly temper his sneer.

'What about him?'

'You knew him when you were at Kerslake,' Fabian told him.

'I knew lots of people at Kerslake.'

'But we understand you took him under your wing?'

Singleton glared at Banner. 'Who told you that?'

'That's not important. But we've just come from Kerslake.' She undid her coat.

'So Wisher told you?'

Fabian briefly met Banner's eye. 'No, Wisher is dead.'

Singleton took that in, his expression unchanging. 'Since when?'

Fabian wondered if it was an act. 'Since he committed suicide five days ago.'

Singleton darted his eyes between them both, as if they might be lying. If it was a performance Fabian thought it was a convincing one.

'Suicide?'

Fabian nodded. 'That surprises you?'

'So why have you come here? You're going to try and pin it on me?'

'You were close to Wisher at one time?' Banner attempted to defuse his aggression.

'Close. No. We spoke but I wasn't his big buddy or anything.'

'That's not what we've been told. There have been insinuations. About the two of you.' Fabian didn't really believe what Compton had told them but knew he could use it as a way to get to the truth behind their relationship.

Hostility hardened in Singleton's blue eyes. 'That's bullshit.'

'Then set the record straight, what was the nature of your association?'

'We talked. That's all.'

'About?'

'It was private. What the hell do you need to know for anyway?'

Fabian cut straight to the chase. 'Did you talk about getting out, and what would happen when you did?'

'Probably.'

He persisted. 'And Wisher didn't ask you to do anything for him on the outside?'

'Like what? Dig up a tin box under a tree? This ain't *The Shawshank Redemption*.'

'No. Kill somebody.' Fabian gauged his deep frown. 'Was that ever part of your private chats?'

'Why would he ask *me* to do that?'

Singleton had never been convicted for murder but Fabian knew he was implicated in several incidents where rival gangs had suffered fatalities in a turf war with the Prentice brothers. 'Did he?'

'No.'

'And the diary?'

He fixed Banner again. 'What diary?'

'The one he kept while he was in prison,' she said, as if it were common knowledge. 'When did he show it to you?'

He scratched the stubble on his neck. 'Don't know anything about any diary.'

Fabian shook his head. 'So, you're going to have no problem accounting for your movements on the 29th and 31st of October?'

'Imagine I was working.'

'Let's try to be more specific. The 29th was Monday. Where were you that afternoon?'

'Monday,' he exhaled at Fabian. 'Think I was in Coulsdon.'

'Think?' Banner took out her phone.

'Pretty sure I was. What was the other date?'

'What were you doing in Coulsdon?' Fabian could tell that Singleton was going to make them work for his alibis.

'Repo job. At a block of flats. Chiltern Heights. There were two of us on the job.'

Fabian knew how the Prentice brothers worked. 'You have witnesses who can back that up? Other than your colleague?'

'Just phone the office. They'll confirm it.'

He'd already guessed that answer. 'I'd rather not rely on your employers. Were you evicting a tenant as well?'

'Yeah, can't remember the name. It'll all be documented, though.'

'And the other date, yesterday, around three o'clock?' Fabian waited while he pursed his lips in thought.

'I was probably here,' he eventually replied.

'Probably?' Fabian sighed. 'What were you doing?' He eyed Singleton's closed laptop.

'Just *in*. Hang on, I called my ex-wife to talk to the kids around four.'

'Before we look at phone records there was nobody else you saw that will confirm it?'

Singleton mimicked racking his brains for Fabian. 'Don't think so.'

'Who *does* live downstairs?' Banner folded her arms.

'It's empty.'

'So you were here all alone?' Fabian stated, wearily.

Singleton shrugged. 'Looks that way.'

Fabian glanced at his watch. Were they were wasting valuable time? It was exactly what Compton wanted. 'Did Wisher ever talk to you about the people he knew on the outside?'

'He might have but they were private conversations between him and me.'

Fabian jabbed his thumb at the door. 'We can continue this conversation at the station if you want, while we check out those two dates.'

'No. He didn't.'

'So he didn't mention the people who visited him regularly?' Banner reeled off the names.

'Didn't mention any of those.'

But Fabian suspected he was lying. He was about to press him further when there was a thud from downstairs.

'Leighton?' A male voice shouted up from the hallway.

CHAPTER THIRTY-TWO

Singleton froze but made no move to the door.

'You not going to invite them up?' Fabian whispered, so whoever it was didn't hear.

'Down in a minute!' Singleton yelled.

'Your front door was open! What are you doing up there! We gotta go!'

'Said I'll be down now!'

Fabian caught the trepidation in his voice.

Somebody thumped up the stairs.

'Just a minute! Wait outside!' Panic in Singleton's warning now.

'What are you doing, spanking the monkey again?' the ascending voice joked.

Banner stood back from the door so it could open.

The humour in the visitor's expression evaporated as soon as he saw the two officers. He was short and thickset and wearing a grey Superdry jacket. His spiky hair was cut into a V on his wide forehead. 'Didn't know you had company.' From the instant hostility on his face it appeared he knew exactly who they were. 'Should I wait in the car?'

'They were just leaving,' Singleton assured him.

Fabian recognised him. He was one of the Prentice brothers, Glen. 'Not quite yet. Afraid he's going to be late starting work tonight.'

'Anything I can help you with?' Prentice feigned courtesy.

'Absolutely there is,' Fabian answered immediately. 'We're looking for an alibi for Mr Singleton for the fifth of October. He tells us he was doing a job in Coulsdon for you that day.'

'Yes. That's my recollection of it.'

Singleton squirmed. He'd immediately realised that Fabian had given him a different date.

'And you'd have the paperwork for that?'

Prentice smiled. 'I'm sure we could locate it for you.'

Fabian was positive he could. 'Excellent. We'll be in touch, give you plenty of notice, if that's OK with you.'

'Anything else I can assist you with, officer…?' Prentice waited for him to give up his name.

He didn't. 'No. Leighton's got everything covered for us.' Fabian raised his eyebrows.

Prentice regarded Banner and then beamed at Fabian. 'I won't be far away.' He nodded at Singleton, turned and left the room.

Singleton let his footsteps reach the hall. 'Happy?'

'Sorry, have we made things a little awkward with your employer?' Fabian closed the door tight. 'I'm sure he realises you're assisting us with an investigation, not that we have any sort of long-standing relationship.'

Singleton grinned humourlessly at him.

'Although he must be wondering exactly what we're talking about up here. I'm sure you'll be able to placate him but the longer you take to tell us about Wisher the more he's going to be using his imagination.'

'Whatever you think you're achieving here, it's not working.' He tried to appear unperturbed.

'Because you're so thick with the Prentice brothers? Quite a staff turnover they have, from what I understand. And very little to speak of in terms of a severance package.'

Banner recited the names of Wisher's visitors again. 'Anything further to add?'

'We don't want to hold you up but, like I say, we could continue this at the station. They have better coffee making facilities there.' Fabian indicated Singleton's dilapidated kettle.

'Are you arresting me?'

'No but I'm sure if we hang out with you all night we just might find a reason to.'

'You're welcome to come along any time.' Singleton spread his hands at Fabian.

'Not sure your boss would be as keen. Or you could save me time and tell us anything you know about Wisher's contacts outside the prison.'

'There isn't anything to tell.'

'You might think so but this is a murder inquiry. Anyone he said was particularly disposed towards doing exactly what he wanted?'

Singleton sighed heavily at Fabian. 'They all would have. 'Cept maybe for his girlfriend.'

'Which one?'

'Naomi Peel. She just wanted to get inside his head. They'd had a thing before and she couldn't let it go. Even after he was convicted. Think she just got her kicks from having slept with him and the fact she was still breathing. He was fixated on her too.'

'What about Ronan Fuller?' Banner asked.

'The author? I think Chris just liked the attention.'

'You think Wisher was an egotist?' Fabian continued.

'He was a pervert. That's why he used to put his hand inside people. Said it was because he was the first to ever touch that part of them. That it made them his, having his hand there before everything went cold. Sounded fucked-up to me but I think it gave him a sexual thrill.'

'Did he talk about dead birds?' But Fabian thought Singleton's mystified reaction was genuine. 'What conversations *did* you have? Did he ever talk about anyone else on the outside?'

'No. He talked about the guy who arrested him the most.'

Fabian said nothing. Did Singleton really not know? He hadn't bothered to look at his ID downstairs, though.

'Not as if he resented him. He wanted to feel that the guy had been rewarded for capturing him. Said it should have sent the copper big places. From what he understood though, from the information he'd got from his visitors, it didn't seem that way. That pissed him off.'

Fabian met Banner's eye and it was obvious they were sharing the same thought. Was this why the diary had been written? Was it Wisher's reward to him?

CHAPTER THIRTY-THREE

When Fabian and Banner left Singleton's home, Glen Prentice was parked up outside in a gleaming red Range Rover Velar SUV with the driver's window open. It was positioned below the orange glow of a streetlight behind Fabian's car and there was a gap of less than a foot between his front bumper and the Audi. He made no attempt to conceal his observation of them.

'Leighton's quickly getting dressed then he'll be hurrying down,' Fabian informed him before they got in. He pulled away and, in the rear-view mirror, saw Singleton leaving the house and approaching the SUV.

'That's going to be an interesting car share.' Banner was looking in her side mirror.

'Feels like we should get to know the Prentice brothers some more.'

'From what I understand they've been under surveillance since May.'

'Who told you that?'

'Snell. Metcalfe's new golden boy.'

Fabian turned the corner and lost sight of the SUV. 'Handy. If Singleton *was* working for them on the 29th and 31st we'll know for sure then.'

Banner pulled on her belt. 'So, how much more d'you think Singleton was withholding?'

'They obviously had some cosy chats. Did he seem genuinely shocked when I told him Wisher was dead?'

'Difficult to tell. But what he told us about Naomi Peel seemed to fit with what we've learned about her already. And we know that Wisher had the serious hots for you.'

'And I thought this was all about Wisher needing to be in the spotlight.'

'Looks like he wanted your promotion more than you do.'

Fabian couldn't stomach that idea. 'Every word in the diary, he's written from my perspective.' That notion was even more unsettling. 'Must be the first time a serial killer has ever tried to empathise with the detective dealing with the crime scenes he's created.'

'But he's only responsible for the blueprint. Somebody else has volunteered to murder on his behalf and they have to be fanatical in the extreme. Maybe we should be looking more closely at the people frequenting the blogs generated by Naylor and Keene.'

Fabian slowed at some traffic lights. 'Finch and McMann are trawling but getting the personal details of anyone is going to take time we don't have.'

'Interesting what he said about Ronan Fuller.'

'Has he sent that first draft manuscript or the audio files over yet?'

Banner checked her emails on her phone. 'Nothing.'

'Let's chase that up.'

Banner nodded and then froze. 'Looks like we're getting a warning.'

Fabian saw she was peering in her side mirror again. He looked in the rear-view and clocked the red SUV behind them. 'Maybe they're just headed our way,' he said dryly.

The Range Rover accelerated so it was again less than a foot away from the Audi's bumper.

Fabian pulled over, dropped his window and waved the car on as soon as the lights changed.

It remained where it was and Fabian could clearly see Singleton seated next to Prentice. He gestured again.

The car revved a couple of times and then glided past them.

'Subtle,' Banner commented.

'Let's have a word with Snell as soon as we can. If he's already keeping tabs on Prentice that's one less headache for us.'

'You think we can dismiss Singleton?'

'Not yet. But I don't want to leave dirty footprints in another investigation.'

CHAPTER THIRTY-FOUR

How long had their lips been together? Tilly had suspected their feelings would overpower them tonight and it felt right to let them. They were all alone in her digs, the only lights were the votive candles on the dresser and they'd just finished a bottle of red wine.

Mark's weight pressed down harder on her as he shifted and his mouth slid down to the side of her neck.

She was ready to let go but sensible Tilly still had her foot in the door. *Has he brought protection?* If she left that question unanswered much longer she doubted she'd be able to prevent herself from being completely irresponsible. But she didn't want to ruin the moment. Things were occurring naturally. Nothing like how it had been with her previous boyfriend, Toby. Maybe she should just let it happen, just this once.

Mark's hand slid under the edge of her blouse and coasted up her side, his fingers coming to rest on her right breast so she could feel the warmth of his palm through her bra.

She opened her mouth, allowed what had been building inside her to be released. Her fingers were in his hair and she pulled his head closer to her. She was so comfortable with him.

A croak escaped his lips as they briefly lost contact with her skin.

But they quickly locked back onto her and she could feel some of the gentleness being replaced by urgency. Sensible Tilly told her these were the moments that could change the course of everything she'd planned.

He was positioning himself now, his kisses uninterrupted while his body slid between her legs.

Tilly wanted to close her eyes and let the sensations wash over her but sensible Tilly folded her arms. 'Wait.'

Mark's attentions intensified. He'd heard her but tried to persuade her otherwise.

And she was momentarily prepared to let that happen. But sensible Tilly raised a disapproving eyebrow. 'Wait.'

Mark shook his head and more of his weight bore down on her. 'Wait!'

The urgency in her command made him freeze. 'Am I hurting you?'

'No.' *Far from it.*

He sighed. 'Are you OK?'

'Have you got something with you?'

'Of course,' he said against her neck.

The buzz of his voice on her throat resonated down her spine. And his response and what it meant should have just salvaged the moment. But she wondered if it was only that which had given her cause to halt things. Even though she was so relaxed. The wine always did that to her. It was almost as if she was sinking into the mattress, though.

Mark moved further down so he was at her shoulder and his teeth slightly pricked her skin.

There was no reason not to allow it to happen now. But even though the moment was becoming inevitable Tilly couldn't. 'Stop. Mark…'

Again he ignored her.

'Mark!' She attempted to sit up so he had no choice.

He looked up at her in bewilderment.

She'd seen anger flash there first. 'I'm sorry.' *What are you doing?*

'I thought…' he reached for words.

'I do. Really.' So what was her problem? Sensible Tilly had been satisfied. Was it because she'd only known Mark properly a month? Or because even though she felt safe with him she really didn't know that much about him? Or did she still harbour a tiny inkling that he might be lying to her about what he did when they weren't together? That was ridiculous. She'd told herself to stop obsessing. But something about the effortless way he explained away every inconsistency made her slightly uneasy.

'Are you uncomfortable?'

'No.' Now she'd ruined it. The impetus had been interrupted.

He blew out a long breath as if it were wasted steam then sat straight so he was no longer looking up at her.

'I'm sorry,' she said again.

'You can always tell me if you think I'm being too rough.'

'No.' She sat up but it was like she had bricks on each shoulder. The room lurched. 'Whoa…'

'You OK?' There was concern in his eyes.

'Yes. Think I got up too quick.' She waited for her head to clear but sitting up further seemed like a humongous effort. Maybe she'd drank the wine too fast.

'Sure?'

She nodded but wasn't.

'You look a bit pale. Let me get you some water.' Mark got to his feet and walked over to the windowsill where there was a half empty Evian bottle.

She rubbed her eyes and looked at her watch. It was only just after eleven. It was like she'd been asleep and just woken in the early hours. 'Can you open the window?'

'Sure.'

Tilly's eyelids were like weights. What was wrong with her? She looked over to Mark and he still had his back to her. What was he doing? She could see his elbow move as he unscrewed the lid from the bottle but he seemed to be doing it painstakingly slowly. Was that because she was getting dizzier? 'Mark. Can I have that water?'

'Coming now.' His voice sounded far away. He didn't turn.

Creeping panic overcame her. Like he might spin around and have a completely different face.

Suddenly the room was bright.

Mark swivelled and the face was his. But she could barely keep her eyes open. She swung her head to whoever had put the light on. It was Ella.

Her roommate was standing in the doorway. 'Sorry, Till. Didn't mean to interrupt anything. Till?'

'She's completely out.' Ella giggled.

He pulled the duvet gently over Tilly. 'She said she was exhausted.'

'She's been burning the candle at both ends. Studies all day and then out with you all night.'

Mark nodded at her. 'I'll just let her sleep. If she wakes, tell her I'll call her first thing.' But he knew she wouldn't regain consciousness for a good couple of hours. Ella would probably be fast asleep by then.

'I'm so sorry I walked in like that.' But there was more mischief in her blue eyes than apology.

'Looks like she desperately needs rest anyway. I think you did her a favour.' Even though she'd thrown a spanner in the works, he appraised Tilly's red-haired roommate. She was still wearing the dark blue poncho she'd entered in, jeans that were ripped over one knee and black leather boots zipped tightly to her legs. Tilly had told him all about her and how she was trying to dump her clingy boyfriend at home to free herself up for college. She was much more his type than Tilly and her gaze darted around him as well.

'The bar's still open downstairs if you're at a loose end.' She was only smiling with her mouth now.

Shameless. She was hitting on him while Tilly slept. He was tempted, however. 'Thanks, I'd better go, though.'

'Come on, I can't tiptoe around here all night. I'll wake her if I do.'

That wouldn't happen. The dose he'd slipped into Tilly's wine made sure of that. But there was no way he was about to jeopardise getting another opportunity. 'I'd really be grateful if you could keep an eye on Till.'

Ella breathed through her nose and nodded irritably.

'I'm sure she'll be fine but it did seem to hit her suddenly.' He tried to appear appropriately mystified.

'So what are you doing for the rest of the evening, Mark?'

She obviously wasn't unclamping her teeth just yet. 'I'll just walk myself home. Was nice meeting you.'

She grimaced and suddenly she didn't look quite so attractive. 'She rehearses the phone conversations she has with you, y'know. I've heard her. Like she's leaning lines.'

'I think we all do that.' *What a bitch.*

'You'd better go then. I'm going to the bar anyway.'

'You're not going to keep an eye on Till?' He already guessed the answer.

She snorted and picked up her handbag.

Wow, she was an ugly human being. No chance she was going to even worry about Tilly let alone question why she'd lost consciousness.

'You gonna put your boots on?' She nodded at his socked feet.

He did and she waited in silence. Was this how it was for Ella's boyfriends when she'd finished with them?

'Come on then,' she said when he'd barely straightened. 'I want to lock the door.' She seized the handle and held it open.

He took one last look at Tilly.

'I think she can manage without you,' she said icily.

He walked out and into the corridor. He didn't even glance at the fire exit as he passed, the one he'd planned to take Tilly down to the Lexus that was waiting in the rear car park. He heard the door slam and Ella's boots pounding behind him.

He thought about Ella in the chair. Locked away with him in the woods. Maybe she would be a good dry run. He would have no compunction testing the tools on Ella. She was by the fire exit now. He could easily ram her head into it and then push her down the steps and straight into the car. He knew there were no security cameras in the corridor.

But Tilly had seen Ella arrive before she'd passed out. If Ella went missing the focus would immediately be on him.

Ella caught up and strutted by.

He marvelled at her skills on her spiked boots. 'Good hunting.'

She didn't turn back but headed down the stairs and he took his time leaving the building.

Ella was just crossing the quad to the student facilities building on the west side. He made his way to his car, opened the door and sat in the driver's seat. He sent Tilly a text for her to find when she woke up.

You were bushed! Me and Ella put you to bed then Ella made a move on me! She's a fast worker. See you tomorrow night. xxxx

He hoped that would misdirect Tilly away from the fact she'd blacked out. Nothing had changed. Everything was still in place for Friday evening.

CHAPTER THIRTY-FIVE

'Fabian, a word?'

It was just after ten on Friday morning and Fabian turned to find Metcalfe standing behind his chair, hands on hips. 'Shall we step in here?' Fabian indicated the glass walled conference room in the corner of the office and Metcalfe strode ahead to it.

Metcalfe entered, shut the blinds and waited for him to close the door. 'I hear you've been talking to DI Snell.'

Fabian had seen this conversation coming. 'He's got the Prentice brothers under surveillance and I needed feedback on Leighton Singleton.'

'And?'

'Singleton wasn't in Coulsdon on a repo job when he said he was.'

Metcalfe was impassive. 'That's hardly surprising, given his record since he got out of Kerslake. He's hardly going to let us know his real movements. Don't worry though, Snell is watching him closely.'

'Not closely enough by the sound of it.'

'He can't monitor their whole operation and Singleton is slippery. It's in hand though.'

'Sounds like Singleton is being allowed to run rings around everyone.'

'Snell is holding back so he can get to the Prentice brothers. I know it's frustrating.'

'It's more than that.'

Metcalfe nodded. 'Snell's in for the long haul and we've invested a lot of man-hours in this.'

Fabian noted the significance of the word 'we.'

'The Prentice brothers know they're being watched and are pursuing their legitimate interests while people like Singleton continue to take care of the real business. We're giving it time, letting them get complacent.'

'How long can that continue, though?'

'We'll get Singleton as well. He's been strong-arming for them but nobody will testify against him.'

And Snell had filled Fabian in on how his strong-arming had put multiple tenants in hospital. 'I suppose you want me to steer clear until I hear otherwise.'

'No. You've interviewed him. You have to follow up but give him the impression you're making headway elsewhere.'

Fabian felt a stab of irritation. 'You're prioritising Snell's surveillance over my murder investigation?'

'Of course not. I've told Snell to accommodate you any way he can.'

'But I'm to stay away from a prime suspect.'

'Is he really?'

'He was one of the few people Wisher confided in at Kerslake.'

'But he was released last year. Did Singleton visit him?' But Metcalfe already knew the answer to that.

'No. But that makes me even more suspicious of him. They were chummy at Kerslake but there's no record of any contact since.'

'Inmates forge friendships inside for survival. Doesn't mean they continue them on the outside. What about your other suspects?'

'We've caught up with ourselves regarding Nadine James. Ainsley Naylor's gaming alibi checks out and several members of Jennifer Keene's swimming group have vouched for her.'

'What about this author writing a book about Wisher?'

'We're chasing him for his manuscript but he has an alibi from his family and nanny. We're waiting to hear back from The Veridian

Hotel about Naomi Peel attending her conference in Frankfurt and Sean Coles was at the restaurant he told us he was at with his friend, Julian Waters.'

'Any witnesses come forward for the O'Rourke murder?'

'No and I don't think they will. The killer is choosing the locations as carefully as Wisher did.'

Metcalfe looked distracted.

Fabian sensed the bad news wasn't over. 'What is it?'

'I've also had a call from Matt Briant.'

'What did he want?'

'He's not happy with the way you and Banner have been conducting yourselves at Kerslake.'

Fabian puffed out air. 'Specifically?'

'He said he's done everything in his power to facilitate you but that he feels his staff have been unfairly treated.'

'I think Briant's just paranoid about the situation reflecting badly on him.'

'Wisher's suicide?'

'Yes. Briant's doing a difficult job but I think Wisher's presence clouded his judgement. I spoke to Wisher's therapist, Doctor Irvine, and I think she and Briant were economical with the truth about how he was handled there.'

'Why?'

'Wisher wanted to transfer to Bicknell but I think they wanted to keep him at Kerslake.'

Metcalfe snorted dismissively. 'For what purpose?'

'I'm not sure but I feel like I need to interview them both again.'

'Your focus should be on catching this copycat not investigating the practices at Kerslake.'

'The two are interwoven. Wisher had to convey the instructions of the diary to someone on the outside.'

'His visitors?'

'Possibly but they're the most obvious choice and I've eliminated all of those except Naomi Peel. Her alibi may check out but we have to consider that the visitors could still be the go-betweens for Wisher and another individual.'

'Exactly.'

'But the staff at the prison are no less likely to have been involved.'

'Are you saying Wisher didn't commit suicide?'

'I believe he did. It was part of his plan, particularly after his diagnosis. But he may have had help securing the plastic tie he hung himself with and, if that was the case, what other assistance did he get? Sounds like the diary was out of his cell for a week before it reached my hands.'

'But Wisher gave it to you.'

'Via two officers on the east wing, Keith Barclay and his superior officer Geoff Michaels, then Matt Briant. I also haven't spoken to the doctor who diagnosed Wisher.'

'Are you telling me you're going to interview everyone Wisher came into contact with during the three years he was in prison?'

'Until I have a solid lead on the killer.'

'Don't neglect your crime scenes. And don't harangue Briant about his personal life.'

Was that it? Were Metcalfe and Briant in the same secret hand-shake club and had just had a cosy conversation? 'I think that was Governor Briant getting a little oversensitive.'

Metcalfe waved his hand. 'Whatever. But the killer is out on the streets, not at Kerslake.'

'But his instructions originated there.'

'That may be but Wisher is dead and Briant is going to be under a lot of pressure. Just be mindful of that.'

'I certainly will be, sir.' Fabian wondered if there was to be more than two wrist slaps.

'Just tread carefully, Fabian.'

'I expect you've already told Briant I will.'

Metcalfe eyed him distrustfully. 'And if you need Snell's input again come to me first.'

CHAPTER THIRTY-SIX

'An old friend to see you.' Finch ducked his head through the conference room doorway as he said it and then met Metcalfe's eye. It was clear he hadn't realised Fabian was talking to him.

Metcalfe waited for him to continue.

'Sorry, I didn't realise you were in the middle of something.'

Fabian guessed that whoever it was clearly wasn't someone Finch wanted to reveal in front of Metcalfe. 'I'll be done in a minute.'

'It's OK, we're finished here.' Metcalfe eyed Finch suspiciously as he breezed out.

Fabian waited for Metcalfe's footsteps to clump back into the corridor to his office. 'Who?'

'Angelina Friedmann.'

'She's here?'

'Downstairs and won't take no for an answer. I didn't think you'd want her on the floor.'

'Thanks.' If Finch had brought her up when he'd been arguing with Metcalfe that would have made matters even worse. 'I'll deal with her.'

He headed downstairs. She'd given him an hour just before they'd spoken to Compton and he'd forgotten to return her call because of Singleton. He found her seated at reception. She got to her feet as he approached.

'Tom.' She greeted him with a half-smile.

He didn't return it. She was clutching a foldable umbrella and wearing a tan raincoat darkened and glistening from the rain she'd walked in from. Angelina had lost weight since they'd last met. Her face was immaculately made up and she'd had her hair dyed a yellow blonde and cut into a neat bob. She was only about five feet tall but her height belied a determined and formidable individual.

She kissed him on both cheeks. 'I assumed I didn't need to take off my coat. Shall we have a little walk?'

'Angelina, I'm very busy. You should have called.'

'I did. Five minutes?' She gestured to the door where the rain was falling hard against the glass.

'It's tipping down.'

'Shall we find somewhere here then?' She raised her neatly trimmed eyebrows.

Fabian didn't even want to be seen with her in the canteen and she knew it. It would get back to Metcalfe. It probably would anyway but better to get it over with. 'Five minutes. But there's really nothing to discuss.'

Angelina didn't reply, simply made for the entrance. It slid open as they reached it and she shot the umbrella. It extended and unfurled and she raised it high so he was sheltered as well. She walked them down the steps and into the car park.

Fabian guessed it was a ploy. He already felt as if he were colluding with her.

'The day Wisher died the channel approached me to do an updated edition of *Urban Predator*.'

But Fabian was positive there was going to be more to the conversation than that.

'You saw Wisher just before he died?'

'Yes,' he answered warily. 'Whoever it is you have feeding you information is definitely worth what you're paying them.'

She glossed over the accusation. 'How was he?'

'Succinct,' was all he would give her.

'He must have had something to say to you. Why would he summon you otherwise?'

'I guess he was just missing me.'

'I can actually believe that.'

'Look, even if I wanted to, I can't have you and your crew as part of this investigation.'

'I wouldn't be. But I have a new reporter. I really think you'll hit it off with her.'

'I'm sorry, this has to be a very short conversation.'

'She'd be unobtrusive. I'd make sure of that.'

'Look, Angelina, you probably know better than me that the climate here isn't going to allow a repeat of the access you had before.'

'If you need me to speak to Metcalfe…'

'No,' he refused flatly. 'That's an ever shorter conversation.'

'You have to recognise how *Urban Predator* was instrumental in Wisher's capture. If the show hadn't aired you wouldn't have had the anonymous witness come forward.'

She was right. 'You don't have to convince me of that, but Metcalfe still resents the spotlight that was put on the department.'

'How can publicising an arrest and conviction be a bad outcome?'

'You know as well as I do that the stats for the department were put into sharp focus. Wisher was a success story amongst a stack of unsolved cases that you also highlighted.' They'd reached the main entrance and Fabian led her out and into the high street.

'Coffee?' She gestured to a café on the other side of it.

'No. This is as far as we go.'

'I want my full five minutes.'

'There's nothing more to discuss.'

'What about the diary?'

Fabian sighed. 'You push like that and you're going to expose your informant. Only a handful of personnel were privy to that information.'

'Relax. Nothing stays inside Kerslake.'

Fabian wondered if she'd been talking to Michaels or Barclay or even Briant.

'And I do know about Nadine James and Polly O'Rourke, remember.'

Fabian suspected that was coming. 'And what about the next victim? Know who they're going to be?'

'Let me help you.'

'If Metcalfe hears I'm talking to you somebody else could be taking my place and I can't allow that. Back off from this. You'll only be jeopardising my investigation and endangering people in the process.'

She shook her head. 'You know I can't step away.'

'I don't understand. You got the promotion you wanted. Isn't this a rung you've already cleared?'

'I'm personally connected to this story, Tom. I have to follow it to the end.'

'The story *has* ended. When Wisher died.'

'But this is his premeditated legacy.'

How much did she know about the diary? 'Sorry, but I have to end this dialogue.'

'I can't ignore my instincts, Tom. We'll do this with or without you but I wanted to approach you out of courtesy.'

'You have done and now you know my position.'

'We've obtained a copy of the diary.' She studied his reaction.

'Is that a bluff?' But having interviewed Briant, Michaels and Barclay about the journey of the diary he couldn't be sure. 'I'm surprised you didn't visit Wisher as well.'

Her expression didn't alter.

'But I know for a fact you haven't.'

'Not in person.' She left that dangling.

Another bluff? Fabian wondered if Ronan Fuller was happy to give up his work in progress for a price.

'But I've kept tabs on him, monitored him since his incarceration. Follow-up is what a good journalist does. You're against the clock now, we can pool information.'

'If you're withholding any…'

'Please. Let's take that speech as read.'

'I'm going back to work now. I really do suggest you drop this one but I know you'll go ahead anyway.'

She nodded. 'I won't hold you up any longer then.'

He turned to the entrance.

'Tom?'

He spun back to her.

'Remember the day you knocked on Wisher's door? How he welcomed us all into his home like he'd been waiting for us?'

Fabian felt the rain fall hard on his scalp.

'Everything was perfect. For you *and* me.'

'What are you saying?'

She opened her mouth and then seemed to stop herself. 'Wouldn't you like to have that again?'

He didn't need to answer that. It had been a pivotal moment for both of them. The culmination of all the months they'd spent in each other's company.

'I can do that for you again. I promise.'

He didn't doubt her certainty but Fabian knew there was very little she wouldn't do to achieve it. 'You were at my shoulder then. This time I feel you might be waiting for me at the crime scene.'

'You've got my number. Call me if you come to your senses.' She turned on her heel and headed across the road.

Fabian watched her black umbrella bounce away before pedestrians and traffic swallowed her up.

CHAPTER THIRTY-SEVEN

When Fabian got back to the office, Banner was seated on the edge of his desk looking uptight.

She stood as he entered. 'Can we talk?'

'Sure.' This sounded serious. He nodded at the conference room and they both made their way there. Had Banner heard about Friedmann's visit and wanted to warn him off? She'd never been comfortable with the journalist hovering on the fringes of the Wisher investigation but had recognised how the exposure had been instrumental in his capture.

She closed the door after her and took a breath. 'Greg has Parkinson's.'

Briefly, Banner reached for the name. He had so many of them churning in his head but then realised she was talking about her husband. Words stalled.

She caught his expression. 'It's OK, I'm still processing this myself.'

Greg Banner, the man his DS rarely spoke about. He and her son were her only family, though. She had to be worried to be sharing with him.

'He's been having tests. Now there's no doubt. I've just got off the phone to him.'

Fabian could tell she was in shock. 'Sit down for a moment.'

'I'm fine.'

'Sit down.' He pulled out a chair.

She sighed, as if he were making too much fuss.

But she sat and he could see the distress tightening her face. 'What about Jonah?'

She shook her head. 'He senses something's wrong...'

Greg was considerably older than Banner and the Dean of Engineering, Design and Physical Sciences at Brunel and their son was showing great academic promise. How would this affect their future plans?

'That's a conversation I have to have with him this evening.'

Her son was in high school. Fifteen – that awkward age. He recalled it was how old Tilly had been when he and Harriet had separated. He'd hated doing that to his daughter but they'd both known it was in her best interests in the long run. But this was a wrecking ball.

'We've only just remortgaged to pay for the extension.'

Fabian could see panic darting her eyes. 'Just hold those gates closed a moment.' He knew she'd have a million thoughts zipping through her brain. 'You're a police officer. You have to be methodical about this.'

'I may lose him,' she said, as if it was the first time she'd spoken it out loud.

That was a truth not easily dismissed. What could he say? 'You have to be realistic. But you've got to make room for optimism as well. What about treatment?'

'I've been researching it, every drug and therapy. But there's no standard treatment. Experiences of the disease differ.'

'So, you can't rush to any conclusions.'

'Greg is strong.' She nodded.

So did Fabian. But Fabian didn't know Greg. Had never met him.

'He won't let something like this beat him.'

'You need to talk to him about this. Now.'

Banner regarded him as if he were insane. 'I'm not stepping away from the investigation.'

'I'm not asking you to. But I will understand if you need to take some time. And you will today. Go home. You have to.'

Banner started to protest.

'Let's save time and say you've refused my suggestion a few times and I've then told you it's an order.'

Banner took off her purple specs and pinched the bridge of her nose. 'But tomorrow is the 3rd – that's when the next murder is due to take place. I *have* to be here.'

'Exactly. I'll need you focussed and you won't be able to do that if you don't work things through with your family.'

Banner put her glasses back on and nodded.

He'd appealed to her logic and knew she couldn't argue with that. 'You've always supported me when I've had family issues. I'm embarrassed to think about how many of those conversations there's been. Just get your stuff and go. I'll speak to the others.'

Banner rose and straightened. 'Thanks.' She briefly made eye contact and then left.

Fabian watched her get her bag and coat from her desk and walk uncertainly out of the office. Finch called after her but she didn't respond. Fabian guessed she was trying to hold it together. She had to be with her family. He'd learned that was more important than anything else.

CHAPTER THIRTY-EIGHT

Fabian and McMann took the lift to C6 West in Frithfield Hospital. Doctor Patlow was on his rounds and the receptionist at the oncology clinic had said that's where he'd be.

McMann enquired at the nurses' station at the front of the ward and a freckled girl who looked too young to be working there pointed them to one of the private rooms. 'Thanks.'

A short man in his forties wearing a white coat with spectacles perched on his forehead emerged as they approached.

'Doctor Patlow?' Fabian asked before he could turn down the corridor.

The man halted and squinted at them. He was losing his dark hair but was still cultivating the fine hairs remaining on his bare scalp. 'Yes?' He squinted harder then pulled his blue glasses down over his eyes.

'I'm Detective Inspector Fabian and this is Detective Sergeant McMann. Is there somewhere we can talk?'

He nodded and gestured them to follow him to the small room opposite. There were a few rows of chairs and a TV inside. He raised his bushy dark eyebrows.

Fabian registered the exhaustion on his face. 'I understand you treated a prisoner named Christopher Wisher?'

Patlow closed one eye then nodded. 'I remember him, of course.'

'Are you aware he'd committed suicide?'

Patlow's expression said he wasn't. 'That is unfortunate.' He sounded genuinely dejected. 'When?'

'October the 27th. You *really* weren't aware?'

'No. I've scarcely been outside this ward for the last week.'

'You can corroborate that?'

He frowned. 'Why would you ask that?'

'Because we have to.'

'My office is a floor below this. Speak to my receptionist about my rota. Now that's a crime scene. And you should see the next seven days.'

Fabian thought he looked as if he'd been on his shift for as long. 'Do you have time to answer a few questions about him?'

'As much time as I normally have. What's this about?' Patlow sat heavily on one of the red plastic chairs.

'We'll get to that.' Fabian stepped back to the door and closed the noise of the corridor out. 'You obviously knew who Wisher was?'

'Yes. He was always accompanied by two guards.'

'How many times did you see him?'

Patlow blinked rapidly and breathed in as if it were a big ask. 'About a dozen times, I suppose.'

'And you diagnosed his brain cancer?'

'Yes. He was very philosophical about it.'

'So his prognosis wasn't good.'

'It was an aggressive glioma, fast growing and inoperable. He was already experiencing severe headaches from the pressure caused by the tumour. I could only offer him pain relief.'

'So he was in no doubt that his time was limited.'

'I told him six months but that his condition would only worsen. I was quite surprised to still be seeing him after that time.'

'Did he discuss anything else with you?'

'Outside of his treatment?'

Fabian nodded.

'No. He was a very… contained person, emotionally and physically. I remember the way he held himself, stiff in the chair, straight-backed throughout, asking pertinent questions and listening intently to the answers I gave him.'

That was a familiar image to Fabian. 'He didn't mention how he was being treated at Kerslake?'

'No. In fact, I don't think we ever acknowledged his incarceration.'

'Did you have any dealings with a Doctor Irvine?'

Patlow frowned.

'His therapist at Kerslake.'

'No.' Patlow shrugged his whole body and seemed to be getting restless.

'What was your conversation about the last time you saw him?'

'Would have been several months ago. I was just monitoring him and adjusting his dosage.'

'So the pain was getting worse.'

'He said it was. And that he was getting blackouts and sporadic vision loss. His main complaint was ringing in his ears. It's common when a tumour is pressing on the temporal lobe.'

'So he asked you not to share the diagnosis with his family.'

'He was very insistent about that. He did tell me that he had other friends to support him, though.'

'Did he mention who?'

'No. Were the circumstances of his death suspicious?'

'Why would you ask that?'

'Why would you be here otherwise?'

'I just want to talk to all the people he came into contact with. He's left a diary behind and we think he may have conveyed the contents to someone outside the prison.'

'A diary? I think he mentioned that. I thought he might be keeping a record of his symptoms.'

Fabian shook his head. 'Did he say anything else about it to you?'

'Not that I recall.'

'Can you remember the guards who brought him?'

'It's usually the same guy from Kerslake.'

'You can't remember their names?'

'Michaels is one. He usually has somebody else to back him up.'

'Barclay?'

'Don't remember.' Patlow got to his feet. 'Do you need me for anything else?'

Fabian could see he was eager to get back to his rounds. 'Thanks for your time, doctor.'

Patlow walked to the door, opened it but paused. 'There was one odd detail I do recall.'

'What was that?'

'He gave his tumour a name.'

'What was that?'

'Bruce. Said it was perfect.'

'Did he tell you why?'

'Never did. And I won't know now.' He turned and strode into the corridor.

Fabian looked at McMann.

'Doesn't Ainsley Naylor call himself Bruce online?'

Fabian nodded. But he was also thinking about Michaels and whoever he had with him transporting Wisher to the hospital. It was at least a half hour journey from the prison to Frithfield. He wondered what their exchanges had been throughout.

But time was ticking by. At what hour tomorrow would the next diary entry become a reality?

CHAPTER THIRTY-NINE

Tilly opened her eyes but could only do so halfway. Something was pressing against them. Something sticky that secured her lashes so she couldn't close them again.

Where was she? She racked her brains to remember where she'd been previously but came up blank. She tensed her wrists but they were secured. It felt like she was sitting up and they were bound firmly to cold metal arms. Panic ballooned. Tilly tried to move her legs but they were tied at the ankles.

She yelled for help, expecting to be gagged but her voice sounded loud in whatever space she was in. Where the hell had she been? Her brain wouldn't give it up. What was her most recent memory? Mark. She was meant to be meeting him. Had she made it to the date? Tilly took a gulp of air and could smell a damp wood aroma. She cried out again and then heard a door open and felt a draught of chill breeze before it slammed shut.

Her breath halted in her throat. 'Who's that?'

Nobody responded but they were definitely standing in front of her.

'Mark? Is this a sick joke? Untie me.'

But whoever it was didn't move from the doorway. Maybe it wasn't Mark. Had she been grabbed after she'd been with him?

'Mark, is that you?' Still no response but Tilly could discern their breathing. 'Please, answer.' Her voice tremored.

Footsteps. Moving from left to right. Their shoes scuffed and hissed on the floor and then stopped behind her.

'Say something. Where am I?' The hairs on her neck stood up. Felt like they'd leaned down to her.

'Are you comfortable?' A male voice said close to her ear.

It was unmistakable. 'Mark?'

He didn't reply.

'Whatever the hell this is, untie me right now.' But she already suspected this wasn't a prank.

'Think it's time you used my real name.'

She twisted her limbs but there was no flexibility. Tilly tried to free her eyelashes from whatever was constricting them but only succeeded in sticking them further so they were open and the rough blindfold was against her eyeballs.

'My name's Liam. And I don't read chemistry.'

Tilly fell silent. Tried to slow the blood coursing through her ears. Whatever she was doing here she couldn't get free. She could only wait for him to explain.

'D'you want to get all the screams for help out of the way?' There was no humour in his voice. 'We're on abandoned private land. It's why I haven't gagged you. I could do though, if that's what you'd like.'

Tilly shook her head.

'Try a scream for size.'

'I believe you.'

'Try one. Easier we get it ticked off.'

'I said I believe you.'

'Shout help. Loud as you can.'

'Mark, what is this?'

'It's Liam. Shout help or I'll cut your nose off.'

The blood started pounding again. 'What do you want with me?' She modified the aggression in her voice.

'Shout. Help.'

Tilly complied and the word rang in her ears afterwards.

'Fill your lungs, Till. Do it properly.' Briefly he sounded like Mark again.

Tilly did so and screamed help as loud as she could.

'D'you hear that?'

Tilly strained her ears. She could faintly make out the swish of distant traffic.

'The M5, probably seven miles from us and nothing but derelict land in between. But I don't want to make this any harder than it is so don't scream again. You'll need all your strength.' He circled around to the front of her again.

'What is this?'

'"This" is something you've been destined to be part of for the last three years. So don't kick yourself for allowing it to happen to you. You were always going to find yourself in this chair.'

'And what… why did you choose me?'

'You're daughter of TV's Tom Fabian,' he said derisively. 'And I'm a big fan of *Urban Predator*.'

But Tilly knew immediately which Liam would want to go to the lengths he already had. 'You're Liam Wisher?'

'Fast. I could have milked that a little longer.'

She had to think rapidly. 'My father put yours in jail. That must have been… I can only imagine how that must have felt.'

'That's right. You can only imagine,' he retorted trenchantly. 'But let's ditch the faux sympathy.'

She couldn't believe she'd allowed herself to be deceived by him. 'I didn't put him in jail. What will any of this achieve?'

'I wish my motive was more sophisticated but it's actually the most obvious one.'

She didn't want to ask. Already knew what it was.

'You're the most precious thing in the world to him. That's why you're in the chair and not him.'

Tilly swallowed hard. 'What are you going to do to me?'

'Out here, on our own... anything that takes my fancy.'

Liam looked down at Tilly Fabian, her eyes held closed with black duct tape and the same binding her hands and ankles to the leather chair. 'I like you though, Till. Didn't think I would but it's good because we're going to spend a lot more time together.'

She didn't answer him but he could see her jaw throb as her teeth clenched.

Tilly had been easy to take the second time. Ella had been out for the night and he'd dosed Tilly's wine again. The darkness had afforded him cover from the rear of the building to his waiting car and he'd carried Tilly there upright. A little like she had when she'd thought he was drunk. 'You've been more than accommodating.'

'So, the night before last. You drugged me then too?'

'Yes. Ella saved you. You can thank her for coming back early, even if she did hit on me.'

'What time is it?'

He hadn't expected that question. 'Why?'

'I want to know how long I've been out.'

'Maybe a couple of hours,' he lied. She'd been unconscious for over seven. He'd tied her wrists and feet before locking her in the boot but had still made sure the dose he'd given her was more than enough for the drive to the farm.

'Untie me.' Tilly looked up at him then, as if she could make eye contact through the duct tape.

He regarded the trolley beside her. She had no idea of the potential pain that its contents could inflict.

'Let me walk out of here—'

'And you promise you won't go to Dad? You promise you'll get me some help? Yeah?'

'No. I promise I won't harm you.' Her concealed gaze remained unwavering.

This was a girl with fire in her belly. 'Thanks for offering that up. And I'm glad you already realise that it's going to be futile trying to appeal to my better side.' Her posture in the chair was combative, her glare still trying to bore through the blindfold. It was an act. She had to be terrified.

'You think my father will allow this?' Tilly said, levelly.

'Your father is going to be busy with other things. Although I should tell you that he sent you a text last night.' Liam plucked her phone out of his back pocket and read it out to her. '"*Don't forget to call Mum. Kiss, kiss.*"'

'This isn't you. It's idiotic. Untie me.'

'You have no idea who I am, Till. You certainly haven't studied me as much as I've studied you.' He went to her photos. 'I did memorise your code when you entered it. Some nice pics of the two of us here...'

'So all this time, every moment we spent together...'

'Yes. There was never a second when I wasn't thinking about now.'

Tilly inhaled sharply, as if to control her emotions.

He punched up the number for Dad, speed-dialled and put it on speaker so she could hear it ring.

'Who are you calling?'

'Tilly?' Tom Fabian picked up after three.

Liam saw Tilly open her mouth to scream and cut the call.

'Dad, help me! Wisher's son has kidnapped me!'

'Good, all the relevant information there. 'Fraid I hung up, though. Do you think he'll call back? Any conscientious father would.'

Her phone rang and she held her breath.

Liam held it close to her ear. She flinched against the loud ring tone. 'Better answer it. Last chance to talk to Dad. No? I will then.' He dropped the mobile and stamped it against the cement floor with the heel of his boot. After the fourth strike it stopped ringing and the screen shattered. 'Looks like we missed him.'

Tilly was breathing erratically.

Liam picked up the phone and used his key to remove the sim. It appeared the severity of her situation was sinking in. 'We never did have the dinner I promised you last night. Think you should at least try to eat something now.'

'What the hell do you want with me?' The hostility had all but left her voice.

'I want you to keep yourself healthy, Till. Otherwise you'll never be able to make it through the first day let alone the rest of the time I've got planned for you.'

CHAPTER FORTY

'Has there been a development?' Doctor Irvine seemed agitated to have Fabian and Banner in her pastel consulting room a second time. Her blonde hair was no longer tied in a band but draped about her shoulders.

'We're actually here to speak with a number of people but thought we'd see if you had some time for us too.' Fabian had been informed that Michaels and Barclay were doing inspections but wanted the opportunity to question her again.

'I've got a major backlog, which is why I'm working Saturday. Is this going to take long?' She displayed none of the composure she had the last time. They had deliberately arrived unannounced, though.

'We'll be as quick as we can,' he assured her.

She seated herself in her chair and gestured them to the chaise longue. Fabian and Banner sat.

'Sorry if we're disturbing your lunch.' He indicated the half-eaten sandwich on the coffee table.

'Just squeezing it in before my next patient.' She said irritably, obviously eager to have their dialogue done.

'Do you normally eat in here?'

'Yes,' she answered wearily, as if it were entirely irrelevant.

'Not with Matt? He mentioned that he sometimes has lunch with you.' Fabian watched her gaze harden.

'What is this about exactly?' She demanded frostily.

Fabian crossed his leg. 'Perhaps you can tell us what your relationship is with him.'

Her attention darted to Banner and back again. 'And what has that to do with Christopher Wisher's suicide?'

'You were both responsible for his Bicknell review. Was it something you discussed outside of Kerslake?' He waited as she considered her reply.

'It's no secret we were seeing each other. Not to anyone here. Everyone gossips.'

'A secret to us, though,' Fabian pointed out.

'Like I say, what relevance does it have? Matt's married. We hardly want it out there and to be an issue for his family.'

'You said "were seeing each other."' Banner interjected. 'Does that mean it's over?'

She nodded once.

From her reaction Fabian guessed it wasn't. 'What happened?'

Doctor Irvine blinked testily at his question. 'Like a lot of these situations… sometimes you reach an impasse.'

'And was that *your* situation?' he pushed.

'Not exactly.'

He didn't give her time to think. 'What then?'

'It's still on and off. I know there's no future in it though…'

'But when it suits you both…?'

She narrowed her eyes at him. 'It's not a crime.'

'Indeed. So do you see others when things have cooled? When Matt goes back to his family?'

'Who I see outside of Kerslake is my business.'

'But what about inside?'

She pursed her lips, frowned and slanted her head.

He took her theatrical bewilderment as an admission. 'Was there more to your relationship with Christopher Wisher?'

Her Adam's apple bobbed silently in her throat.

He'd suspected she'd been concealing something the first time they'd interviewed her. 'Was the attack on you purely because you'd turned him down for Bicknell?'

'Yes.'

'Or did he know that the two people who made the decision were sleeping together?'

'That decision was entirely objective.'

'But it certainly suited Matt Briant's agenda, to have a high-profile prisoner like Wisher remain in his prison. Or did he have more personal motives for wanting to keep him here? Did you have a sexual relationship with Wisher?'

'I told you. He was fixated on Naomi Peel.'

'I know how Wisher works, how skilled he is at making you think he's opening up exclusively to you. Did you submit to your curiosity about him? Ask yourself why he would still use the memory of his ex-mistress to fulfil himself sexually when an attractive woman like you was sitting in the room?'

The doctor closed her eyes and inhaled.

'Doctor Irvine?' he prompted.

'There was an isolated incident.'

Interesting terminology, Fabian thought. 'You were intimate?'

'I… it was a regrettable decision.'

'But you continued offering him therapy afterwards?' Banner failed to keep the incredulity out of her voice.

'I knew what he'd done. Knew he'd manipulated me…'

'During or afterwards?'

Irvine shook her head at Fabian. 'He was still my patient.'

'Who were you seeing first, Wisher or Matt Briant?'

Irvine frowned.

Fabian knew why Banner had asked the question.

'Wisher,' Irvine admitted.

He thought as much. 'Did you punish him for duping you by turning him down for Bicknell?'

'No,' she retorted flatly.

'Or were you still fascinated by him?'

'That decision was reached principally because he didn't fit Bicknell's admission criteria.'

'"Principally?"' Fabian repeated. 'And nothing to do with the fact that Briant may have had a problem with one of his inmates having sex with you before him?'

'I never told Matt.'

'Like you say, "everyone gossips", though,' Banner reminded her.

Fabian raised his eyebrows. 'It's very likely, as governor, that it would get back to him. Did you really not tell him? Or was denying Bicknell by colluding with Briant your way of chastising your patient for pulling your strings?'

'No.' Irvine folded her arms.

Fabian speculated what would have happened to Wisher if he'd ended up at Bicknell. But his cancer diagnosis would have been the same. 'So how long did it take before Wisher found out about you and the governor?'

'I never told him.' She leaned rigidly back in her chair.

Fabian persevered. 'You didn't take great delight in telling him or at least intimating that you would never sanction his transfer because of what he did to you?'

She was silent.

Fabian took that as a yes. 'Was that the reason he attacked you?'

'He was a violent man.'

'Not inside. Only on that one occasion. You said he was "courteous, respectful".' Banner fed back the words the doctor had used in her previous interview.

Fabian sighed. 'Doctor Irvine, according to Wisher's diary somebody else is going to be murdered… today. I've already been to two crime scenes so if you're concealing anything more that's been going on here than your unprofessional conduct with a patient and your superior I want you to tell me right now.'

Doctor Irvine eventually shook her head. 'That's it. I've told you everything.'

'And Matt Briant will confirm this?'

She looked at him with resignation. 'Yes.'

'This is a disciplinary matter that will have to be pursued in due course but if you're absolutely sure you've got nothing to add that will help my investigation, that will shed light on Wisher's diary...'

'No.' She focussed on the carpet. 'I know Matt was worried the diary was Wisher's attempt to disgrace Kerslake, which is why he wanted to read it before it was handed to you.'

'Michaels and Barclay, any dealings with them?'

'I know them more by sight than anything else.'

'OK. I'd appreciate it if you didn't contact Briant until we have.'

She reluctantly nodded.

'Think she told us everything?' Banner's heels clunked as they headed along the metal gantry towards the east wing.

'My instincts tell me she has. She had to hide her liaisons to protect her professional reputation and I believe Briant is doing the same.'

'So we *don't* need to interview him again?'

'Not immediately. It's an internal inquiry now.'

'So you're prepared to believe that Briant got hold of the diary and held onto it for a number of days only because he was afraid it could compromise Kerslake?'

Fabian looked down to the inmates standing outside their cells awaiting inspection on the level below. 'He's said nothing to make us think otherwise. I believe he's been trying harder to keep his affair with Doctor Irvine out of the investigation.'

'What about Michaels and Barclay?'

'I want to speak to them now. Find out how cosy they got with Wisher when they were transporting him to Doctor Patlow.'

'You really believe they could be Wisher's link to the third party outside the prison?'

'The alibis for our other candidates are stacking up.' Again Fabian wondered how to ask Banner about the outcome of her family meeting the day before. She'd gone out of her way to avoid the topic on the drive to Kerslake.

She halted at a door and waited for a guard to unlock it. 'What about Doctor Patlow? I'm still waiting to hear back from Finch on his background check.'

'We saw the rota. He didn't have time to grab a coffee let alone murder two people. He's not top of my list but we're not dismissing anyone.' Fabian took out his phone to try Tilly again. Why had she called him early that morning and hung up? Had she pocket dialled him?

But it immediately rang and he answered.

'Another one's been found,' McMann said sombrely.

'Where?'

'Turner Grove Plant Nurseries. Dead bird at the scene.'

CHAPTER FORTY-ONE

'Eat it.'

Tilly kept her lips closed against the cold chicken nugget Liam was pressing to them.

'If you don't eat I'll sling it out the door and you can starve.'

She could smell the greasy breadcrumbs against her mouth but kept her jaws clenched shut.

'Think you'll have anyone else bringing you food? Open up.'

Tilly still didn't obey.

'OK. That's your first and last chance gone.' He took the nugget away.

'Wait,' she said as she could hear him move towards the door.

His feet hissed as he turned on his heel.

'I'll eat.'

'Too late now.' But he didn't move.

He was right. She was completely dependent on him and had to eat. Hadn't since the previous lunchtime. Had expected to be dining with him on their date. Her stomach was grumbling around nervous acid. 'Please.' She listened to him breathing.

'Barbecue or ranch?'

'What?'

'Which dip would you like? I've got both here.'

'Just give me the food.'

She felt the nugget at her lips again and opened her mouth. He pushed it in and she robotically chewed on the clammy and salty processed meat. Terror had been replaced by resignation and

Tilly was now thinking logically about what to do. Staying alive was her first priority.

'There's twelve pieces here.' He pushed in another.

She hadn't even finished chewing the first. Her mouth was parched and even though her stomach was empty her constricted throat pumped against the food.

'Chew on them. You'll salivate more.'

'Wait.' She retched.

'Here.'

She felt a straw to her mouth, the end of it pricking her bottom lip. 'What is it?'

'Sprite. Sorry it's not a Scarlett O'Hara.'

'What have you put in it?'

'Don't worry. You're where I need you. And now I want you awake. Sip it.'

She still didn't take the drink. But the nuggets were like a dry pulp in her mouth.

'Come on, Till. I'll take it away in five, four, three, two—'

Tilly sucked on the straw. Her mouth filled with cool, sugary liquid. Could she detect another taste? She didn't drink Sprite. Her reflex was to swallow it but she held it there as it fizzed around the masticated food.

'Tilly…'

She allowed it to slide down and she'd barely drawn breath before he forced another greasy nugget in.

'Let's get this done now,' Liam said sternly.

What choice did she have? Maybe the Sprite was just that and it was actually the food that had been sprinkled with something. It was the only sustenance she could get, though. Tilly ate the next piece and was able to chew it more easily.

He fed her three more until her mouth was full and then the straw butted her chin again. 'Give me a moment…' she said through her full mouth.

'Just eat faster.'

She tried to but it still felt like she was trying to ingest cardboard.

'Enough then?'

She nodded as her stomach spasmed. He kept the straw there and she took another sip.

'OK, dinner done, greasy chops.'

She felt him wipe a napkin around her mouth. He pressed harder, his fingers clamping it to her lips so she started to suffocate. She tried to yank her head away but he held her fast, the paper covering her nostrils as well.

'Just making sure you're cleaned up for the camera.' He grunted as he kept it in place.

Tilly could feel her circulation start to pound in her brain and tried to thrash her body in the chair, instinctively lifting her hands to protect herself but they only moved a couple of centimetres from the arms.

'You've still got it around your mouth.' He gripped her face tighter.

Tilly yelled against the gag. Felt her hot breath heat her chin.

Liam pushed her firmly against the headrest of the leather chair. 'Let me get that for you.'

Tilly strained for air and her stomach convulsed as he squashed her nose. Blackness crowded in. 'Let me go!' The words were crushed and incoherent in her head.

But he didn't and the sounds of her pain and panic drained away.

Liam felt Tilly's body slacken. It was only a matter of seconds before the lack of oxygen to her brain would cause more damage than he wanted. He held her for seconds longer. Counted. Released her on three.

Tilly tugged in a faltering breath and choked back the food. She jerked her head to the side so he couldn't pin her again and the Sprite streamed and bubbled out of her nose.

'And I'd just got you cleaned up. Now I have to start all over again.'

'No!' She shook her head violently.

Liam lightly dabbed at her face with the napkin and she twisted her head back and forth as she anticipated more of the same.

'Just take five. I'll be back soon.' He dropped the napkin onto the trolley beside the nugget box and walked out of the lock-up into the clearing under the horse chestnut trees. It was a dingy day and the ground frost still hadn't melted. He put up his hood, took out his phone and dialled.

'What is it now?' The voice the other end barely concealed their irritation.

'I'm killing time here.'

'And that's all you have to do. How is she holding out?'

'She's just had dinner.'

'Good. Give her what she needs but don't let her talk you into anything.'

'I was thinking of giving her a little walk around the forest.'

There was no response.

They still didn't realise when he was joking. 'Course I won't. She's not going anywhere.'

'Just don't give her the opportunity to worm her way around you.'

'You know what a soft touch I am,' Liam said scornfully.

'You've been intimate with her. Don't let that cloud what you've got to do.'

He sucked in the cold air through his teeth. 'Just focus on your own itinerary.'

'I have been, which is why we can't afford any unnecessary slip-ups now.'

'We can always swap roles, if you don't trust me to look after things here.'

The person on the other end of the call sighed. 'I didn't say that. I'm just emphasising we both need to stay alert.'

'Thanks for the pep talk.'

'And stick to the B roads if you need to drive into town.'

'I have been.' Liam kicked at a dried-out conker shell.

'Nobody has seen you use the private road?'

'I'm putting the chain back each time, as instructed. You're sure nobody from Matlin is going to come sniffing around?'

'The sale is still being negotiated. There shouldn't be any more surveyors there for another couple of months.'

'There was a truck at the dairy yesterday.'

'That might be the Goldbrook people emptying the milking sheds so they can auction the equipment. Just stay on the east side and don't touch Fabian's girl until I get there.'

He mumbled a response.

'Liam?'

'Yes, OK,' he snapped and looked back to the lock-up.

'It's been a while.' The voice was placatory. 'Just be patient.'

Liam considered who lay only feet from him and how the person on the other end of the line was powerless to stop him doing exactly what he wanted to her.

'Everything has to be done at the right time. Fabian has to see it on-screen.'

The tools were laid out. The end result would be the same. Liam wasn't frightened of the consequences of improvising.

'Liam?'

'I'm here.' But this was his father's wish and he owed his loyalty to him, if nobody else. 'I'll wait.'

'Just keep her alive and secure in the meantime.'

'The media haven't connected the murders yet.' Liam heard the drizzle start to land on the hood of his coat.

'It's going to happen.'

'No mention of the birds.'

'The police are withholding it. But they won't be able to for much longer. Just sit tight.'

Liam lifted his face and allowed the cold moisture to fall against it. 'Things are contained here. It's more likely *you* that's going to make a mistake.'

'Not so far. Just remember, you're Tilly's nurse at the moment. When I get there, and only when I get there, that's when you get to be something else.' The speaker hung up.

CHAPTER FORTY-TWO

Fabian pulled his Audi into the small car park of Turner Grove Plant Nurseries just off Streatham Common. A uniformed officer waved them through and they halted in one of the few spaces left. A group of around twenty people were gathered by the entrance to the retail cabin and crime scene tape had been stretched across it. An ambulance was positioned nearby.

He and Banner got out of the car and hastened to where another uniformed officer was dealing with the disgruntled customers.

One woman was getting very agitated. 'How much longer do we have to hang around here? I have to pick my daughter up from ballet.'

'Make sure you get statements from all of them,' Fabian said as he and Banner lifted the tape.

They paced through the small shop and then out of another wooden door to the grounds behind. There were three main greenhouses on the gravel plot and beyond that eight poly tunnels stretched away in the adjoining field. They crunched their way to the next uniformed officer they saw and he directed them into the far greenhouse.

Inside the atmosphere was like a humid July day and the smell of the flowers and plants positioned on long tables was overpowering. Mills was at the far end of the third row with his three-man team, all dressed in white and, in the surroundings, reminded Fabian of a group of silent beekeepers.

Fabian located a box of foot covers and they both slipped theirs on before joining them. As they approached Fabian knew who they were working around. It hadn't been confirmed but it looked like the owner of the nurseries, Bridget Pearce, was the victim. He saw the soles of her trainers first and then spotted the yellow evidence cone nearby. Miniature pots and soil were scattered around the area.

Mills turned, didn't greet them and stepped back to reveal the body. The woman's arms were arranged above her head, her eyes were closed but her mouth was open and teeth clenched. There were blood spatters over her face. Fabian calculated her to be in her forties, she wore a turquoise headscarf, also spritzed red, a sage green gardener's apron and blue jeans. The front of the apron was soaked through with dark stains and a large pool had leaked from her slashed throat, trickled a couple of feet and almost reached a stack of terracotta pots against the rear of the greenhouse.

Mills ran his hand over his bald pate. 'Three deep stab wounds to the neck, chest and abdomen. There was obviously a struggle.'

Fabian examined the slits in the apron. 'Abdominal trauma?'

'Looks that way. And I've barely finished with Polly O'Rourke.'

'Who found her?'

'Her business partner, she's still in shock. The paramedic is with her.'

'Approximate time of death?'

'Think she's been lying here a good few hours. According to the FOA her partner said she comes in at six to start work. It was sometime between then and the other members of staff arriving but this greenhouse isn't open to the public yet so nobody came back here until lunchtime.'

Fabian turned to the dead bird beside the cone.

'He's gone exotic with this one.' Mills indicated the green parakeet.

'There's a plentiful supply in London,' Fabian commented dourly.

It was obvious the animal's neck had been crudely twisted. Fabian scrutinised the concrete floor. 'Any prints in the soil?'

'Couple of indentations. Might be partials but he probably exited down the other aisle.'

"*No real tears yet.*" Fabian recited the entry and bent to study Bridget's face. 'Are her eyes intact?'

'Yes.' Mills confirmed.

"*I'm going to be moved tomorrow though. Have to trust them.*" He repeated the remainder of Wisher's words for that day.

Banner carefully joined him. 'Is he talking about the body being moved?'

'They're meant to be my thoughts. *I'll* be moved tomorrow.'

'Physically, emotionally?' Banner speculated.

'What do I "trust?"'

'Instincts?' Mills suggested.

'Or *who* do I "trust?"'

The three of them stood in silence while the three techs continued to work around them.

Mills took out his phone. 'I'll call Lucinda, tell her I won't be home for the rest of the weekend.'

'Can you have the reports on both victims to me tonight?'

Mills grimaced at Fabian. 'Tomorrow morning, with the best will in the world.'

Fabian shook his head. 'Tonight. There's another entry for tomorrow.'

Mills exhaled.

Banner took out her mobile and read the next day's entry from her notes. "*Bird in a cage. Can't escape. But listen. What's a little purgatory between friends?*" It's the most direct reference to you. Or at least the connection he still believed he had with you.'

Fabian cast his eyes around the scene. 'It's an explicit threat. Sounds like he's dishing out a punishment. And whatever it is leaves me "numb" until the 12th. That's when the entries finish.'

'The 12th?'

Fabian nodded at Mills.

'Don't you think that's ominous?' The pathologist's expression was grim.

Fabian had already considered what that meant but turned to Banner. 'Let's talk to Bridget's business partner. Call me when you're done with both.' He left Mills to his work and headed back to the car park.

'So you've considered how much danger you could be in?'

Fabian didn't turn to Banner as they walked back down the row. 'Of course. But if these are my thoughts then I'm still meant to be alive on the 12th.'

They strode back through the shop and encountered the cluster of customers again. The uniformed officer was still trying to calm them.

'Sir?' He called after Fabian as they made for the ambulance.

Fabian stopped and turned.

'That lady over there arrived early for work this morning.' He pointed at a diminutive girl with her dark ponytail sticking out the back of a dirty white baseball cap sitting on a bench beside the trolley bay. 'Said she saw two cars parked here. One was the victim's, the other she didn't recognise.'

Fabian made a beeline for her.

She looked up as he approached and wiped a tear out of her eye. She wasn't much older than sixteen.

'Detective Inspector Fabian, you work here?'

She nodded.

'And you are?'

'Angie, Angela Butler.'

'What did you see this morning?'

'Like I told him, I got here about seven to work in the tunnels. Bridget's VW was parked where it is now.' She looked over to it.

Fabian followed her gaze to the silver vehicle.

'And there was another car parked over by the entrance.'

'What sort?'

'Don't know. Sporty. And it was dark blue.'

There wasn't now. Banner was already scanning the park for cameras. 'No CCTV out here?'

Angela shook her head. 'None inside either.'

'You didn't notice the reg number?' But Fabian already knew the answer to that.

She shook her head again.

'And you didn't recognise it as belonging to a member of staff?'

'No. Nobody else comes in as early as me. 'Cept Bridge.'

'There was nobody sitting in it?'

'No. I walked right past it to get to the side gate. The shop wasn't open.'

Fabian regarded the small wooden entrance. 'And what did you do then?'

'Went straight to the tunnel.'

'You didn't see anyone else around?'

'No.'

'Didn't go to the greenhouses?'

'Had no reason to.'

'OK.' Fabian surveyed the car park. 'It's definitely not here now.' He addressed Banner. 'That's a main street outside. It's bound to be covered by cameras. Let's see if we can pinpoint a dark blue sports car travelling along it between six and seven. Get Finch onto it now.'

CHAPTER FORTY-THREE

Liam had drugged the Sprite. Tilly was sure of it. But whatever it was had the reverse effect of what he'd slipped into her wine.

She was now wide awake to every uncomfortable physical sensation she was experiencing – the ache in her wrists from being so tightly secured to the arms of the chair and the blood throbbing against her restrained ankles. Even smell and sound seemed to be heightened, her circulation was thudding faster and she felt that if her senses intensified any further she would be overwhelmed by them.

Alarm bells should have rung the first time she'd blacked out. Even though she'd been staying up late with who Tilly thought was Mark Mason, she'd never passed out from exhaustion before. But she'd been so incensed that Ella had hit on him while she'd been insensible she'd ignored her instincts. She'd drunk the wine again the next evening. Given Liam Wisher his second chance.

Tilly's eyes felt bruised and the pressure of the tape across them had started an ache in the centre of her forehead. Her mouth was bone dry and her ears were burning. From the acoustics she guessed she was in a small space. She'd screamed for help every time he'd left her there alone but it was clear from the fact that he hadn't used a gag that he was sure nobody was going to pass by.

Liam Wisher had said the noise she could hear was from the M5. Maybe he'd been lying about that. Perhaps she was miles away from Exeter. After all, she had no idea how long she'd been out after she'd lost consciousness.

But she had one thing to cling to. The word 'Matlin'. It was part of Liam's telephone conversation he'd had outside that she'd overheard and Tilly knew it was the name of a big pharmaceuticals company. Sounded like she was being held on a piece of land that the organisation had acquired to develop. And from his side of the dialogue she'd gathered there was a chain across the entrance to it.

Who was the person he was in touch with? She'd assumed this was a one-man vendetta but he clearly had an accomplice and from the tone of the exchange this other person appeared to be calling the shots. And Liam said he was going to wait. For how long? Until his accomplice arrived?

She inhaled and released a breath slowly but it did nothing to calm the racing of her heart. Had he given her speed?

The door opened and she straightened. Did Liam have company now?

'Relax,' Liam said flatly.

'What have you given me?' She could barely break the question out of her throat.

'I'll admit, you're having more than a sugar rush.'

She listened for signs of other footsteps but couldn't discern any as he closed the door behind him.

'Just means you won't miss a moment of the party.'

'Have you spoken to my father?'

'No. This isn't a ransom situation.' His tone was emotionless.

Tilly felt her blood briefly decelerate.

'Why are you going to these lengths?' she blurted out. 'If you do what you're threatening to do you'll be destroying your own life as well.'

Liam took his time considering her question. 'My life was destroyed the day my father was arrested. There was no such thing as normal after that.'

'But my father told me your mother changed her identity. Why didn't you? Start again somewhere else like she did?'

'Because I refused to lose who I was.'

'You would have only had to change your name. Not alter who you were. Wouldn't that have made your life easier?'

'It would have, denying my father. The police told us exactly what we had to do to hide after he was convicted. Warned us what we'd have to face if we didn't. But my father was in so many photos of me growing up. I couldn't burn my existence as well as his.'

Tilly wondered if this really was an opportunity for her to change his mind but suspected he was toying with her again. 'I understand he was your father—'

'Which means you don't. The person I knew hadn't changed. He gave me love and security.'

'But knowing he'd done those things…'

He didn't reply.

She tried to imagine his expression. 'You must have been sickened by that. How could you ever come to the conclusion that my father should be punished for stopping him?'

He scoffed. A short hiss through his nose. 'You really believe it was your father that stopped him?'

Tilly felt a cold current ripple through her.

'Him and Angelina Friedmann? *Urban Predator* and that last-ditch TV appeal for witnesses? D'you think that led to the anonymous tip-off?'

Tilly tried to blink moisture from her eyes and orange dots flickered across her vision. 'You?'

'My father controlled that completely. He told me to do it.'

She swallowed.

'I walked to a phone box. Made the call. I thought the police cars would be parked outside the house when I got back but it was another half an hour before they arrived. I just went up to my room and hit the Xbox. Dad was sitting in the kitchen downstairs, chopping onions for my mother. For a meal he knew he wasn't going to eat.'

'She didn't know?'

'Not until your father knocked the door with the camera crew in tow.'

'But he confessed to you?'

'Santa doesn't exist. Mum and Dad have sex. Just another revelation to deal with on the path to adulthood,' he said, acerbically.

'Why *then*? After he'd killed nine people.'

Liam sniffed.

Was he crying?

'Then your father walks into our home.' His voice had thickened. 'Acts like he's super cop for the cameras when it was me that pointed him there. I never saw my father again after that. They grilled my mother. The papers made every insinuation about her. It was why he didn't tell her anything. He was sure she'd be implicated. But my father knew I'd be spared.'

Tilly wanted to believe he was lying. That her father agreeing to do the TV show had given the investigation the boost it needed. But it sounded like the truth. 'You never visited him?'

'He told me I shouldn't. Ever. That I was only to remember him as he'd been at home. And now he's dead.'

'My dad was doing his job.'

'No. Mine did it for him.'

'So I have to pay for that now?' Her muscles tightened against her bonds and the pain was acute. 'Because my father locked away a man who, according to you, willingly gave himself up?'

'My father was prepared to take his punishment. For the lives he ended and the others he ruined. Your father stole plaudits that didn't belong to him. I spent three years being alienated by people that knew who my father was. But then I found others who were drawn to me *because* of him. I learned that I didn't have to forget him; that I could do something to restore the balance. That if society was to revile me and make me a pariah for the rest of my life I could at least do something to earn it.'

'By killing me?'

'I haven't said I'm going to kill you.'

'Then what am I doing here?'

He said nothing.

She had to talk him round, before his accomplice arrived. 'Whoever it was who came to you, they convinced you to be part of *this*? Can you not think for yourself and see how wrong this is?'

'I did the right thing by my father and it led me to a black despair I know only suicide will end. That's coming soon but before that I want your father to feel the pain of losing someone he loves as well.'

'Who has turned you to this? I refuse to believe that the person you were with me isn't who you can really be.'

'That was role play. That was me trespassing on a life I can never have.'

'But I fell for *you*.'

He snorted. 'You fell for Mark Mason, not the son of Christopher Wisher.'

'That's not true.'

'If you'd known who I was, you would have recoiled like the others.'

'I'd begun to think I was in love with you.' It was what Tilly felt she needed to say. To stay alive. But it was also exactly what she'd been prepared to tell him during the last evening she thought he was Mark Mason. Something she'd be scared to in case it frightened him away.

There was no response.

'*You* were the person I was with, even if you were using someone else's name.' She could hear him move forward and tried to look up at him and fix him with her blindfolded eyes again.

'You'd say anything now.' But his voice was small.

'I don't know what I'd do if you released me now. That's the truth. But I do know that you haven't harmed me yet. I get you don't want me to say that I understand your anger. But I do want to *try* to understand it.'

'Of course you do.' But there was little aggression in his voice.

'Follow your instincts. I know they're telling you this isn't going to make things right.'

He was silent.

The suspended atmosphere was broken by the sound of an approaching car.

CHAPTER FORTY-FOUR

When Banner returned to the office Fabian was again considering how to ask about the conversation she'd had with Greg and Jonah when a call came through from Mills. And having been so hastily summoned, Fabian knew he had to have something significant to show them. Banner followed.

Debbie Chive, the mortuary operations coordinator, greeted them both as they entered the small clinical reception area. 'Go straight in.'

The fact that there was no banter wasn't a good sign. He and Banner went through the doors beside her desk.

Mills was standing by the examining table wearing green scrubs and blue surgical gloves. Bridget Pearce's naked body was laid out, the dark slits in her white flesh cleaned up but the long incision across her abdomen gaping with part of her lower intestine exposed.

'You surely haven't finished your report?' Fabian knew the body would have only just been transported from the scene.

'No but I thought you'd better see this.' Mills used a pair of surgical tweezers to pick up an item from a stainless-steel kidney dish.

Fabian examined the object. 'A flash drive?' The black and silver component glistened wetly.

'It was inside her. Had been pushed into the incision in her abdomen.'

'That's what you had to trust. Guts not instincts,' Banner said, repulsed.

Fabian moved closer to the object.

'Shall we find out what's on it?' Mills indicated the laptop sitting on the desk opposite.

Fabian nodded, sickened anticipation drying his mouth.

'I couldn't find any print traces on the housing.' Mills cleaned the moisture off the drive with a wipe and used the tweezers to insert it into the side of his laptop. He put on a pair of thick-lensed specs and frowned at the screen. 'OK…'

He located the drive and double-clicked its icon. A window opened and there was one file inside labelled:

TILLY

Fabian felt the blood drain from his face. The sound in the room was suddenly dampened.

Mills hit the file and the image inside.

Fabian could see it was Tilly. His daughter was seated in a chair, black tape binding her eyes and securing her hands to the arms.

An incoherent sound escaped him.

'When did you last speak to her?'

But he scarcely heard Banner's question. His attention was locked on the photo.

'What's that say in her lap?' Mills leaned forward.

Fabian focussed on the piece of white card there. There was text:

GOLDBROOK FARM
TALBOT FOREST
OPEN CHAIN TO SERVICE ROAD OFF A379
COME ALONE OR LEAVE ALONE

A phone number was below.

The threat was explicit. Suddenly the sickly sweet aroma of Bridget Pearce's body was overpowering.

'Where are you going?'

Fabian was almost to the swing door.

'Sir!'

He turned back to Banner. 'I have to leave, *now*.'

'Wait.' Mills shook his head. 'You can't do this on your own.'

He pushed on the panel. 'You can read. I'm not jeopardising Tilly.'

'Just think for a moment.' Mills held up his palms.

'I don't have that. If he asks, tell Metcalfe I said I was on my way to his office but left the station.'

'I don't give a monkey's about procedure, Fabian,' Mills snapped. 'You're walking into a trap.'

'They have Tilly. I'm not going to let Metcalfe make any decisions concerning her safety.'

'That's understood,' Banner placated. 'But call the number first.'

Fabian had to go. Didn't want to waste another second discussing it. But he knew Banner would follow and he couldn't risk that.

'Call it now,' she insisted.

Fabian swiftly took out his phone and dialled. It was answered after four rings. 'Hello?'

No response only low breathing.

'I know somebody's there.'

Still no reply.

'I've seen the flash drive. Where's Tilly?'

'Hello, Dad.' It was a male voice, whispering.

'Do *not* hurt her. I'm coming to the location you've given me. My daughter has nothing to do with Wisher.'

Somebody sniffed but didn't react to what he'd said.

'I'll be coming directly. I'll surrender myself to you. But don't touch her. I warn you now, if you do…'

'If *we* do?'

More than one. Fabian met Banner's eye. She was shaking her head at him. 'I want to talk to you. We'll talk.'

'If more than one person passes through the service road gate, she dies.'

'I understand. There'll be nobody else with me.' He avoided Banner's gaze.

'Come and find her...'

'I need to know she's OK.' Fabian waited, expected the phone to be hung up.

'She's alive... for now.'

'Give me proof,' Fabian demanded.

There was a momentary pause. 'OK...'

Fabian gulped solidly and heard the phone the other end thud and then a rustling sound.

There was a low murmur.

'I can't hear what you're saying.' Was that because of the blood surging in his ears?

'Dad?' It was Tilly.

'Tilly.' His vision blurred. 'Are you OK?'

'Matlin site. Somewhere near the M5,' she babbled quickly

'Forget it, Tilly. He knows where we are.' A different male voice said to her.

'Don't endanger yourself. I'm coming to get you now,' Fabian assured her.

'It's Wisher's son,' she said as swiftly.

'Tilly, don't say anything more.' Liam Wisher? Was this plan already fully formed when Fabian had spoken to him recently?

'She's alive, for now.' The first voice was back on the phone.

Was that Liam Wisher? How many of them were there? 'What is it you want from me? I can arrange a payment, tell me how much.'

'No ransom. All we want is your presence. And nobody else's.' They hung up.

'Well?' Banner asked as he lowered the phone from his ear.

'No ransom. And Tilly says it's Liam Wisher. There's somebody else there, though. You have to let me go.' Fabian stated simply.

Banner and Mills were silent.

They couldn't allow it. 'If this was Jonah you'd want me to do the same.'

Banner knew it to be true but said nothing.

'I'm party to this and I can't agree to it, Fabian.' Mills folded his arms.

'Give me four hours. Got to Metcalfe and say I told you we were all to meet at his office at seven. Act surprised that I don't show. That'll give me time.'

'This isn't about our position.' Banner's expression was pained. 'They're going to kill you. Wisher had this planned long before he handed over the diary.'

'Maybe he has something else in mind for me.' But he knew that plea wasn't going to wash.

'All that time he appeared to respect you.' Banner stepped towards him, as if he were about to flee. 'This is what it's been concealing. You took away his freedom, his family. It's what he wants to do to you.'

'Tilly is my only priority.' He couldn't allow her to be bound and gagged for one second longer.

'Phone Harriet.' Banner pointed to the phone in his hand.

'That will only complicate matters. There's no time.'

'Phone her,' she said firmly. 'She deserves to know.'

'I know what I have to do already.' He pushed the panel.

'Then I'll follow you out of that door.'

'Stay put. That's an order.' He held out his hand to her.

'Just think about this for a few more seconds,' Mills cautioned.

But Fabian had already made his mind up. 'Go to Metcalfe now if you want.' He turned to leave.

'Sir.'

But he didn't hesitate. Fabian headed to the car park. He'd call Harriet on the way. Banner was right. She had to know. But nothing she said was going to keep him from Goldbrook Farm.

CHAPTER FORTY-FIVE

'You're not thinking straight.' Harriet's voice teetered between anguish and panic.

Fabian kept his foot on the accelerator. It was getting dark and his Audi hadn't left the fast lane since he'd joined the M4. He'd just missed a flight from London City Airport to Exeter and there wasn't one for another four hours. He could drive there in three and a half. 'There's nothing else to think about.'

'Where's Banner?'

'She tried to stop me when I left. But I can't put Tilly's life in Metcalfe's hands.'

'Will she go to him?'

'I don't know. I'll find out when I get to Exeter.'

'And what are you going to do if you're alone?'

'Reason with Wisher's son.'

'But you said there's more than him involved.'

'Whatever the agenda, they want me present.'

'How did Tilly sound when you spoke to her?' Harriet's question dried.

'Petrified.'

'Are you armed?'

'Of course not.'

Neither of them said anything as Fabian negotiated the lights of the cars in front. There was nothing *to* say. He was doing what any parent would.

'I'm coming too,' she said eventually. 'Give me the location.'

'No.'

'Tom!'

'The best thing you can do is be ready for Tilly to come home.'

'I need to be there. This isn't only your decision.'

'Yes it is.' He hung up and took out his earpiece.

The phone started ringing immediately. He switched it off.

It was pitch black when he reached the service road to Goldbrook Farm and he very nearly missed the exit. His satnav told him he'd arrived at his destination a few moments before and as he sharply swung the Audi onto the gravel track the headlights illuminated the gate across it.

Fabian jumped out of the car and felt for the lock at the post but his weight swung the gate wide. He pushed it the rest of the way and drove through. No sign of any police vehicles. Looked like Banner and Mills had given him the time he needed. They would have been trying to call him too.

He followed the camber of the track, the Audi bouncing and crackling, its lights shifting solid shadows in the trees either side. All he had to focus on was finding Tilly. He would beg, plead for her release; do whatever was necessary to secure her freedom.

Several minutes later the beams lit up the side of a small cinder block building in a clearing. No glow from inside. He eased the car to a standstill outside but left the engine running and the headlights on. They knew he'd pulled up and he prayed that no police cars were about to bring up the rear.

Fabian got out and closed his door. He gazed into the darkness of the forest, took out his phone and switched on the torch. The beam barely extended to the fringe of the trees. Anyone could be watching him from in there.

He peered up as a helicopter puttered overhead. Please don't let that be NPAS. Fabian waited but the sound of the rotor faded so only his engine filled the atmosphere.

There was little point in delaying what he'd been asked to do. They had Tilly. He had to follow instructions.

Fabian walked to the dirty yellow wooden door of the building and pushed it inwards, breath loud in his ears and heart pumping his throat. He shone his torch inside and played it across the chair that Tilly had been secured to. It was empty. Some strips of black tape hung from the metal arms.

He felt a sharp pain in the back of his leg. Looking down he angled it and saw what looked like a red flower head behind his knee. It was a dart. He spun around and looked back at the car but the headlights dazzled him. Nobody there.

'Where is she?' He directed the demand into the blackness behind the Audi and his words sounded sluggish. 'I've come alone.'

Fabian dropped to one knee and tried to get up again. He staggered back against the half open door and felt it swing all the way inwards and then a hard impact to his shoulders.

Footsteps on gravel. But they faded as they reached him.

CHAPTER FORTY-SIX

When Fabian woke he was looking at a cracked ceiling. He sat straight, felt his brain catch up with the action and held onto the edge of the bunk he was on. He was in a tiny windowless cell. A small, old-fashioned lamp with tassels hanging around the edge of the purple shade was positioned on a small stand beside a tiny TV set. Next to the stand was a commode. There was no other furniture in the room. He checked his pockets. No phone, wallet or keys.

Fabian got dizzily to his feet and tried the handle of the galvanised steel door. It was locked. He noticed another handle in the middle of it. He pulled it down to reveal a metallic recess, which was empty. Looked like a chute for depositing items from the other side. He closed it and banged on the panel. 'Let me out of here, now!'

He heard footsteps echo down a corridor.

'If you need water there's a bottle of Evian by the bed,' a courteous male voice said.

'Take me to Tilly.' He fought to keep the anger out of his voice.

'You'll see Tilly in a few moments.'

'Now,' he growled.

'Demands aren't yours to make. I've told you, you'll see her soon.'

'Where is she?' Fabian tried to glimpse him through a gap around the edge of the door but couldn't discern any light the other side.

'Nearby. But you're not in Goldbrook Farm any more. We've relocated you.'

'Liam?'

'Tom.'

'What do you hope to achieve with this?'

'Just redressing a balance.'

'By throwing your life away? Open the door. It's not too late to salvage this.'

'It *is* too late. For you, and me,' he declared assuredly.

'So, you're going to lock me up?'

'Yes.' Liam replied, simply.

'But my colleagues know you're part of this. Think you're going to evade capture?'

'Worry less about me and think more about the choice you have to make.'

'And what is that?' Fabian felt cold apprehension climb onto his shoulders. He was imprisoned, powerless, and positive Liam Wisher had carefully planned whatever was in store.

'Go to the TV and switch it on.'

Fabian turned to the tiny set beside the lamp and reached it in three paces. He pressed the power button on top.

The screen was activated. Fabian immediately identified who he was looking at and the room shrunk in on him.

The high-def colour image showed Tilly seated in a swivel chair. Her eyes were blindfolded by tape as before, her hands secured to its trunk behind her. Beside her a figure was standing. He wore a papier-mâché mask with crude curls of hair stuck to it, the pink-painted profile approximating Christopher Wisher's impassive expression.

But his eyes were drawn to the trolley of surgical implements positioned beside his daughter.

'Stop this,' Fabian heard himself say.

'There's no sound. No mic. But when it starts, you may just be able to hear her screams. She's in the cell right the other end of the corridor.'

Fabian returned to the door. 'What do you want me to do? Tell me,' he said through gritted teeth.

'Watch.'

He slammed his fist hard against the metal. 'Tilly's not part of this!'

'You know you're not only responsible for punishing the guilty. Families have to suffer,' Liam stated calmly. 'The sentence is theirs as well.'

'If you harm her—'

'If I harm her what? That room is the only place you're going to know now. For the next three years.'

'You can't keep me hidden away here.'

'Nobody knows where you are. You'll see out your time here.'

Fabian took a breath. Knew he had to calm himself so he could think straight. 'Your father took his own life. Why does the suffering have to continue?'

'He took his own life as the first phase of his plan. And I intend to honour it.'

'Why? He's dead.' Fabian said with incomprehension.

'Because he gave himself up to you because of me.'

CHAPTER FORTY-SEVEN

Fabian shifted on the balls of his feet. 'What does that mean?'

'The anonymous caller, the one you probably thought found their courage because of *Urban Predator*. That was me.'

Fabian opened his mouth but no response emerged.

'Nothing you did put my father behind bars. He told me to make the call, give his reg number and say I'd seen the car leaving Justine Kavanagh's address.'

That was Wisher's final victim before his capture. Unease wormed under doubt.

'Why would he do that? And why would you agree?' Fabian looked over to the screen at Tilly. The figure was still standing motionless beside her.

'He wanted to protect me.'

He didn't take his eyes from it. Had to play for time. 'You didn't question what he asked you to do? Even though it meant his imprisonment?'

'Of course. But he told me he had no choice.'

'You knew what your father had been doing, before his arrest?'

'Yes.'

'How?'

'He took me to play golf at a local course. Bought me my own set of clubs. I left them in the boot and one evening I wanted to practise my swing so went to get them out when he was taking a shower. Took the keys out of his jacket pocket and opened it up. I found a polythene bag in there. When I looked inside I found two dead starlings.'

'Your father leaving them next to the bodies of his victims – that detail has still never been released to the public.'

'It was a bizarre discovery to make. Their necks had been almost twisted off their bodies. I didn't get my clubs out. Closed the boot and returned the keys to his pocket. But he knew I'd been in there. He came to me in my room the same night, sat on the bed and told me a story about his mother and father. They'd died before I was born and he'd never really spoken about them. They'd been older when they'd had my dad. As an only child he'd played a lot on his own. He said he always fought a losing battle for their attention. Until he found an injured magpie in the gutter outside their home. The end of its wing had been run over. He'd put it in a fruit crate and kept it in the shed. His parents came to see his patient every day and he'd give them a progress report. It was the attention he'd been craving. My father fed it and nursed it back to health, but he could see that it was ready to fly again. And then he'd have nothing to show his parents. He didn't want to give up their visits.'

Fabian nodded, knew what came next.

'He took his father's hammer and broke the wing again. Kept the bird in the crate. But the bird deteriorated. My father tried to nurse it better a second time but his parents could see that it wasn't going to live. They stopped visiting the shed. He felt guilty, having almost saved the bird and then injured it again. He put it out of its misery. Wrung its neck. That was when he got the most attention. They comforted him. He said it was the one and only time he felt truly loved. He told me that, even as a grown man, he'd never felt that sort of love from anyone. He reassured me then. Held my shoulder and told me that whatever wasn't right between him and Mum, he would never turn his back on me. Then he walked out of my room.'

'Did your mother and father fight?'

'I never heard them argue. Not once. But Mum was always chipping away at him, even though he worked full time and did all the parenting. Everything was under the surface with Dad. I never saw him get angry.'

'Did your mother know who your father really was?'

'If she ever suspected, I don't think she admitted it to herself.'

'So how did you find out for sure?'

'I wanted to know why he kept the birds in the bag. The next time he took us shopping I deliberately left my phone in his car. Stuck it in the pocket on the back of his seat. I had it linked up to my laptop so I could track it.'

Fabian still held his gaze on Tilly. The figure beside her looked impatiently at his watch.

'The afternoon he went to Justine Kavanagh's address I knew he was there. I was meant to be at home revising for an entrance exam the next day but I climbed out of my window and walked over there through the park.'

Fabian recollected the property and what he'd found when he'd got there.

'Dad's car was on the other side of the park but when I reached it I saw him going up the track to the house. There was something in the way he moved. It didn't look like Dad at all. I didn't want to follow. Almost turned around and went home. But I walked up to Justine's.'

Tilly twisted her body in the chair but the figure didn't react, only its papier-mâché face tilted slightly to observe her.

'When I got there I heard Justine screaming and went around the back. She was attacking my father in the kitchen with a saucepan. I thought she was his mistress and it was a big fight. He was almost unconscious on the tiles and she was still hitting him. I yelled at her, told her to stop but she started swinging at me, knocked me onto my back. Dad tried to help, got to his knees and grabbed her but she turned and pummelled him, wouldn't stop. I picked up a heavy wooden chopping board from the side and hit her with it. Hit her until she stopped.'

Fabian heard him gulp and waited for him to continue.

'Dad ordered me to leave the house. To go home and let him take care of things. He didn't return for a couple of hours and when he did he slipped into my room and told me that I was about to find out why he'd been at Justine's and that the less I knew the better it would be for me. He said he was entirely to blame and that the punishment was to be his. He made me promise to follow his instructions to the letter, call the police anonymously and never admit that I'd been at the house. Then he said that once he'd been arrested he never wanted me to look him in the eye again. Wanted to spare me that. He embraced me then and I knew it was the last time. He didn't want me to miss my exam. We had breakfast together the following morning. Carried on in front of my mother like nothing had happened. She couldn't see the raw wounds under Dad's hair.'

Fabian recalled that Wisher had told him he'd sustained the injuries when Justine Kavanagh had fought back.

'I sat my exam, came home and then walked to the phone box as he'd instructed.'

The mutilation to the stomach had been the same. Wisher had stayed behind and made sure Fabian thought it had been only him. 'You were defending your father. You didn't know he went there to murder Justine Kavanagh.'

'But I did soon after. When you walked into our family home that evening and I realised he was covering up more than an affair gone wrong.'

'Weren't you repelled when you discovered who your father was?'

'He kept his promise to me. Never revealed I'd killed Justine,' Liam said sedately.

'And was that enough to make you a willing murderer too?'

'There are many who will gladly hold the knife for my father. But it was one man who visited him at Kerslake Prison who conveyed his plan to the others. My father told him exactly how to interpret the diary he was writing for you.'

'Who, Liam? They've just used you. Used your anger. Tell me who it is.'

'I'm only interested in taking the freedom you stole from my family.'

Fabian didn't blink as he watched his daughter squirm in the chair. 'Do what you want with me, just let my daughter go.' But he'd already realised that Liam knew her suffering was the key to his.

'No. That's your choice.'

'What the hell do you mean?'

'Your first option is that she stays down here with you. For three years. You'll only ever be able to see her on that little screen, though. You'll never be able to communicate with her. Not ever touch her. And she won't be able to see you. We'll feed you both for exactly three years. Then we'll stop. The only thing we'll give both of you then is a plastic noose. You can decide whether to starve or end it like my father did. I wonder what Tilly will choose? Particularly if she thinks she's down here all alone.'

'Tilly!' Fabian yelled. She didn't react. 'Tilly!' He watched the figure select something from the trolley and Tilly's head turn sharply in the direction of the sound. 'Stop him!'

'So maybe her death is exactly what you want.'

The figure was holding a syringe.

'I'll do whatever you ask.'

'My friend could do that for you. It'll be painful to watch, might even take a couple of days but at least you'll spare her three years of misery with only suicide waiting at the other end.'

'Stop him!'

'Think carefully. If you spare her you'll be committing her to the same sentence as you. What's it to be?'

Fabian recalled the diary entry for the day before.

No real tears yet. I'm going to be moved tomorrow though.

And then for today.

Bird in a cage. Can't escape. But listen. What's a little purgatory between friends?

'Get him away from her!' Fabian slammed his fist against the door.

'Everything will happen as my father has dictated.'

The figure flicked the end of the syringe.

Fabian noticed a band of white skin around the little finger of their tanned left hand. 'Please, do anything to me; just leave Tilly alone!'

'I promised him I'd follow his instructions to the letter. Even those I felt it difficult to stomach.'

In desperation, Fabian booted the door under the handle and the impact resonated painfully in his leg.

'But he liked you. Wanted to give you one chance to escape this. One tiny chance.'

'Open this door, Liam!'

'Just calm down and think. I'm going to say this once. And only for his sake. Why did he like you, Fabian?'

He shook his head. Was this a cruel riddle?

'Because you always listened to him. Did you go on listening to him? The last time you saw him? That's going to be pretty crucial.'

Fabian's circulation pounded but he tried to focus on what he was saying.

'Maybe once he was behind bars you thought you didn't have to any more.'

Fabian frantically replayed the last conversation with Wisher when he'd handed him the diary at Kerslake. He remembered him asking Fabian if he was still listening. What the hell had he said then?

'I thought he was wrong about you. That you didn't deserve any of the respect he gave you. Was I right?'

Fabian could see the figure take a firm hold of Tilly's arm and tug back the sleeve of her sweater. 'Stop!'

'And it was right there for you. Get out of jail for you even though he knew *he* never would.'

Tilly was soundlessly screaming.

'Shame.'

'Retrospection!' Fabian tore the word out of his throat.

Liam was silent.

'Retrospection!' He shouted again, his eyes still on the screen.

The figure was bending over her arm and Fabian couldn't see what he was doing with the syringe.

'Retrospection. One word. It's your saving grace. But not indefinitely.'

CHAPTER FORTY-EIGHT

The lock of the door snapped.

A trick?

Fabian cautiously took hold of the handle and tugged. It opened inwards and he was looking into a short gloomy corridor. There were lagged pipes overhead and a few dim strip-lights lit the walls. There was no sign of Liam.

Fabian squinted but could see a swing door at the end. He ran for it and paused, it still hadn't settled in the frame. Liam must have escaped this way. There was no other exit. He couldn't see anything through the circular windows in the black panel but pushed through regardless.

He was in another dark corridor similar to the one he'd just left. There were more swing doors straight ahead and one to his left about halfway up. He tentatively pushed that one first.

He was standing in a small room and Tilly was slumped forward in the chair.

'Tilly!' He ran to her.

'Dad?' she said groggily.

Fabian looked frantically around the dingy space. There didn't appear to be anyone lurking in the shadows but he couldn't be sure. 'Did they hurt you? Did they touch you?'

She shook her head. 'Untie me,' she said weakly.

Fabian started uncoiling the tape from her wrists.

'Please let me see,' she croaked.

Fabian carefully prised the tape from her face.

Tilly squinted against the faint light. 'Where have they gone?' she asked panicked and shot her bloodshot eyes around.

Fabian quickly released her hands from the trunk of the swivel chair and then bent to her ankles. He ripped away the bonds and stood up. 'Can you walk?'

Tilly got to her feet and winced. 'I'll be fine. Let's go.'

They inched into the empty corridor, Tilly limping as the blood fought to get back into her toes. No trace of Liam or the other man.

'Come on.' Fabian escorted her to the swing doors at the end and paused to listen. No sound from the other side. He pushed it. 'Stay here.'

Tilly followed him as he stepped through.

They were now at the bottom of a flight of concrete steps and passages led off to the left and right.

'Daylight.' Fabian indicated the sliver of blue on the wall beside the steps. He looked first at the left then right passages. Where did they lead?

'Quick.' Tilly started to climb the steps.

'Wait!' He went up after her. 'Let me go first.'

The staircase led to a concrete platform and another flight led up from it to the left.

'A door!' Tilly exclaimed.

They could both see the glowing white outline of it above and ascended hurriedly towards it.

But before they reached the panel they could hear the sound of a loud, whirring motor outside.

Fabian butted the metal door wide and had to shield his eyes from the morning sunlight. As his vision became accustomed to the glare he could make out a police helicopter settling in the clearing.

The door slid open and four figures jumped out. One was Banner. She bent low under the blades and scrambled to him.

'Are you both OK?' she shouted over the noise of the engine.

Fabian turned back to check on Tilly.

She nodded at Banner.

Two uniformed men, one of them armed with a rifle and a plainclothes officer joined them.

Fabian leaned to Banner's ear. 'Did Liam Wisher and another man come out this way!'

'No. We've been trying to find a place to land, they tracked you from Goldbrook Farm to here. There's officers at the north exit so they won't be able to escape there!'

'What is this place?'

'It was a slate mine but now it's a UGS facility for gas tanks!' the bald plainclothes officer informed him.

'Dad, stay with me!' Tilly tightly linked her arm to his.

Fabian nodded at Banner that he would stay and look after her.

Banner hastily headed towards the bunker entrance with the other officers.

CHAPTER FORTY-NINE

Fabian pulled the Audi against the kerb and the accompanying patrol car halted behind them. He and Banner undid their seat belts.

'How's Greg?' He'd been circling the question on the drive over to Clapham.

Banner's expression clenched.

But he suspected her usual knee-jerk reaction to him enquiring about her private life was something that would have to change.

Her face softened slightly and she nodded. 'We're taking it a day at a time.'

'That's all you can do.'

'How was Patricia?'

That was one call Fabian hadn't wanted to make but he insisted on breaking the news of her son's suicide himself. When the UGS facility had been searched Banner had found Liam Wisher dead in one of the storage bunkers. He'd hanged himself with one of the plastic carpet ties that his father had used. 'Said I'd meet her when she comes to ID the body. I don't know where I'll begin with that conversation.' Fabian shook his head.

'Deceived by both her husband and son. She doesn't have other family either, does she?'

Fabian exhaled. 'I think she always felt there could be a rec-onciliation with Liam…' How had Liam become embroiled with his father's contrivances when he had never visited him? But there had been no trace in the bunkers of the other man who had worn the papier-mâché mask.

'Come on.' Fabian opened his door. 'He's expecting us.'

They both approached Ronan Fuller's double-fronted Edwardian home, two uniformed officers behind them.

Fabian assumed he would have slipped the onyx signet ring that he'd noted him wearing on their first visit back on his little finger. He'd removed it when he'd been preparing to torture Tilly but because of his tanned skin Fabian had clearly been able to make out, even on the small screen in his prison cell, the white outline of the missing ring on that finger of his brown left hand.

The double garage door was closed but Fabian was sure that one of the three vehicles he'd seen parked inside it previously was the dark blue sports car Angela Butler had spotted in front of Turner Grove Plant Nurseries the day Bridget Pearce had been murdered.

Fabian knocked and Fuller's wife answered the door and smiled. She kept smiling as she showed them to her husband's office for a second time. He could hear the two children laughing and stomping around upstairs.

Ronan Fuller was standing behind his desk and from the apprehension on his face Fabian guessed he knew they weren't there to pick up his manuscript.

'Ronan Fuller, I'm arresting you on suspicion of murder and for the kidnap of Tilly Fabian.'

Fuller was wearing the signet ring but Fabian knew he'd find the white band if he took it off.

'But I've already given you an alibi.'

Fabian continued to read him his rights and wondered at what point he'd crossed the line from analysing Wisher's homicidal motives to becoming the conduit for his revenge. Maybe during their conversations about Fuller's book, Wisher had deftly manipulated him into believing they should collaborate on another.

'Ronan, what's going on?' his wife asked from behind them.

'Don't worry, Lib. Call the solicitor. I'm saying nothing to these two.'

'But why are they arresting *you*?'

She'd given him his alibi along with the nanny and Fabian believed it to be true. Particularly after what Liam Wisher had said.

There are many who will gladly hold the knife for my father. But it was one man who visited him at Kerslake Prison who conveyed his plan to the others.

Others. He wondered how many Ronan Fuller had enlisted to execute Wisher's diary? Fabian was certain it was somebody else who had stabbed Nadine James in Battersea Park. But which, if any, of the suspects he'd already interviewed was it? Or would he have to start an online hunt for other fanatics? Unpeeling their identities there was going to be an almost insurmountable task.

CHAPTER FIFTY

Fabian knew he wouldn't eat breakfast before he sat down at the table in his kitchen. He'd been awake since two and up since just after four. Dread weighed heavily in his stomach and he could only manage a few sips of coffee before he got dressed and ready for work.

Today was Monday November the 12th. The last entry in Wisher's diary that read:

Waiting. Anticipating. Sisyphean sentence continues…

Fabian knew that Sisyphus was a Greek mythological figure who was punished for his self-aggrandising by having to roll a huge rock up a hill only for it to roll back down when it reached the top and having to repeat the action forever.

These were his thoughts and he *had* been waiting. Anticipating being summoned to another crime scene to find Wisher's trademark there.

Ronan Fuller was still refusing to talk. Was it because he knew exactly what was coming next?

He had no choice but to submit to the day's schedule. It was out of his control.

He shaved then called Harriet and told her he'd call in to see her and Tilly on his way to work. He didn't imagine Tilly would return to Exeter for the remainder of the term and the doctor had prescribed her medication he normally would have frowned upon. But she'd been having problems sleeping and the previous evening Tilly had taken the pills and he'd stroked her head while she'd slept for six straight hours on the couch.

But they were lucky to still be a family, to still be together and he reminded himself of what Banner had yet to face.

Fabian checked everything was switched off in the kitchen and was just heading out when somebody rang the doorbell.

He opened the front door, examining the carpet outside his flat as he had every day since the bird had first been deposited there. He descended the stairs to the door in the hallway and could see the postman standing outside. He opened up.

'Package for Tom Fabian.'

He warily accepted the cardboard box. Without thanking him he closed the door on the postman and took the delivery upstairs.

Blood pummelled his eardrums as he grabbed a knife from the drawer and slit along the parcel tape sealing the flaps of the box. But he already knew from the weight exactly what was inside.

Four more A4 diaries and as he opened the 2018 one on top he guessed which would be the first date filled in.

He scraped through the blank pages until he reached November 12th.

Waiting. Anticipating. Sisyphean sentence continues…

… today. And 35 more months to go.

Handwriting filled the following days. Not Wisher's. And not Fuller's. Somebody else's. Cryptic entries to the end of 2018.

He found the same filling every page of the next diary and the next two until October 27th 2021. Every day, without exception.

Over a thousand days. Was this what Wisher had been dictating to Ronan Fuller during his visits for book interviews? Who had Fuller sent the audio files to? They'd not been found at Fuller's home. Perhaps he sent them directly from his phone when he'd sat with Wisher in Kerslake Prison. And perhaps this other individual had stabbed Nadine James in Battersea Park.

Retrospection. One word. It's your saving grace. But not indefinitely.

Wisher had deliberately tantalized him. Only allowed him a brief reprieve. Having been released from his cell Fabian was being put back at the helm of an investigation the serial killer believed him worthy of.

Wisher had escaped his but Fabian had only just started his sentence.

A LETTER FROM RICHARD

Thanks so much for reading. I hope you enjoyed the second Tom Fabian book and that it's left you curious as to what he and Natasha Banner will encounter next. If you want to keep up-to-date with all my latest releases, just sign up at the following link. Your email address will never be shared and you can unsubscribe at any time.

www.bookouture.com/richard-parker

There are more adventures to come and book three will be his most gruelling case yet. If you do have time to rate this book or leave a brief review on Amazon that would really be helpful and very much appreciated. It does make a huge difference. And please feel free to contact me on Twitter, Facebook or Instagram – I very rarely bite.

Richard Parker

 www.richardjayparker.com

 RichardJayParkerFans

 @Bookwalter

bemykiller

ACKNOWLEDGEMENTS

There are so many exciting books out there so I really appreciate you choosing this one, devoting your valuable time to Tom Fabian and bringing it to life with your imagination. As always, love and kisses to Anne-Marie for continually supporting my determination to keep making things up for a living. To the shed and beyond. Eternal gratitude to my Mum and Dad for keeping the scrapbook going! Love you both.

Huge thanks to all the talented folk at Bookouture central. Oliver Rhodes hand-picks the best and they not only know what they're doing but make it inclusive and fun as well. I'm very fortunate to have had the perspicacious editorial talents of Kathryn Taussig guiding me through Tom's second adventure. It's our third book but it's her continued encouragement beyond publication day that I value as much. Kim Nash and Noelle Holten also go above and beyond the call of duty and it's their skills at creating a buzz around my books that are key to every Bookouture author's success. Thanks to other masterminds Natalie Butlin and Alex Crowe for their smart campaigns and ability to keep tweaking and maximising those conversions. See, I almost sound as if I know what I'm talking about. Gratitude to Jon Appleton and Maisie Lawrence for their valuable notes and much warmth to all the supportive Bookouture authors in the lounge. They're always there to boost anyone who's having a bad day.

My work wouldn't see the light of day without the generosity and enthusiasm of committed bloggers who will happily promote authors on Twitter, Goodreads and Facebook for no other reason than they are passionate about the books they read. The importance of this can't be underestimated so heartfelt thanks to anyone who has given up their time to post a review or share them.

These include: Nicki Richards, Jen Lucas, Donna Maguire, Zoe-lee O'farrell, Karen Cole, Nigel Adams, Suze Clarke-Morris, Kaisha Jayneh, Berit and Vicci at Audio Killed The Bookmark, Katie Jones at The Book Cave, Amanda Oughton, Emma C. at Booking Good Read, Sean Talbot, Rachel Broughton, Alison Drew, Magdalena Johansson, Diane Hogg, Renita D'Silva, Martha Cheeves, Joyce Juzwik, Amy Sullivan, Kelly Lacey, Rebecca Pugh, Claire Knight, Chelsea Humphrey, Ellie Smith, Lorraine Rugman, Steve Robb, Emma Welton, Stephanie Rothwell, Cleo Bannister, Abby Fairbrother, Sarah Hardy, Meggy Roussel, Sheila Howes, Linda Strong, Maxine Groves, Joanne Robertson, Susan Hampson, Kate Moloney, Eva Merckx, Jules Mortimer, Mandy White, Malina Skrobosinski, Shell Baker, Mandie Griffiths, Jo Ford, Kaz Lewis, Fran Hagan (right?), Carole Whiteley, David Whiteley, Dave Carr, Dave McNeill, Norma Farrelly for spreading the books around, Tom Bromley for writing his piece in *The Journal*, Doctor Kelvin Jones, Russell Young and Scott Griffin. Apologies to anyone I've missed. Get in touch and I promise to put you in the next one!